Four Seasons of Heythwaite

by

Annie Eileen Rogers

Copyright © 2018 by Wise Grey Owl Limited

ISBN: 9781720074656

All rights reserved. This book or any portion thereof may not be reproduced or used in any manner whatsoever without the express written permission of the copyright owner except for the use of brief quotations in a book review. Published in the United Kingdom of Great Britain & Northern Ireland and subject to the Laws of England and Wales. First Published, 2018.

All characters contained within the book are fictitious. Any resemblance to living people is purely coincidental.

Published for Wise Grey Owl Limited, www.wisegreyowl.co.uk or www.wisegrayowl.com

Dedication

To Harrogate Writers' Circle and the Promoting Yorkshire Authors self help group who gave me the inspiration to complete this novel.

Key Characters

Old Friends and Family

Dolly and Betsy.

Albert (Dolly's deceased husband).

On the Allotment

Harold, Bert and Walter.

Dora (Harold's wife).

Elsie (Bert's wife).

Ambrose and Beatrice.

In the Café – Edwina's Coffee House

Edwina.

Jane (Edwina's Assistant).

In the Garage

Dick.

Luke (Dick's Apprentice).

On the Farm

Alastair (Shaw).

Robert and Amy.

Kit (Amy and Robert's son).

Bouncer (the dog).

At the Hairdresser

Madge.

Introduction

Workmen

Alex and Iggy.

Around Heythwaite

Daniel (Taylor, Trainee Electrician).

Angie (Graduate Engineer).

Irene (Angie's mother).

Allotment Growers Association Committee

Councillor Amanda Braithwaite (Chair).

Annie Taylor (Secretary).

David Wilson (Treasurer).

In Australia

Andrew (Dolly's son) and John.

Diane (Dolly's daughter) and Danny.

Timmy and Joanne (Diane and Danny's children).

Janet (Andrew's cleaner).

Jimmy and Babs (Yacht owners).

Carter (McBride, Jimmy's PA).

Ryan (Jimmy and Bab's son).

Pubs of Heythwaite

The Old Oak.

The Sandpiper.

Optician

Gareth and Julia (Gareth's Wife).

Map of Heythwaite

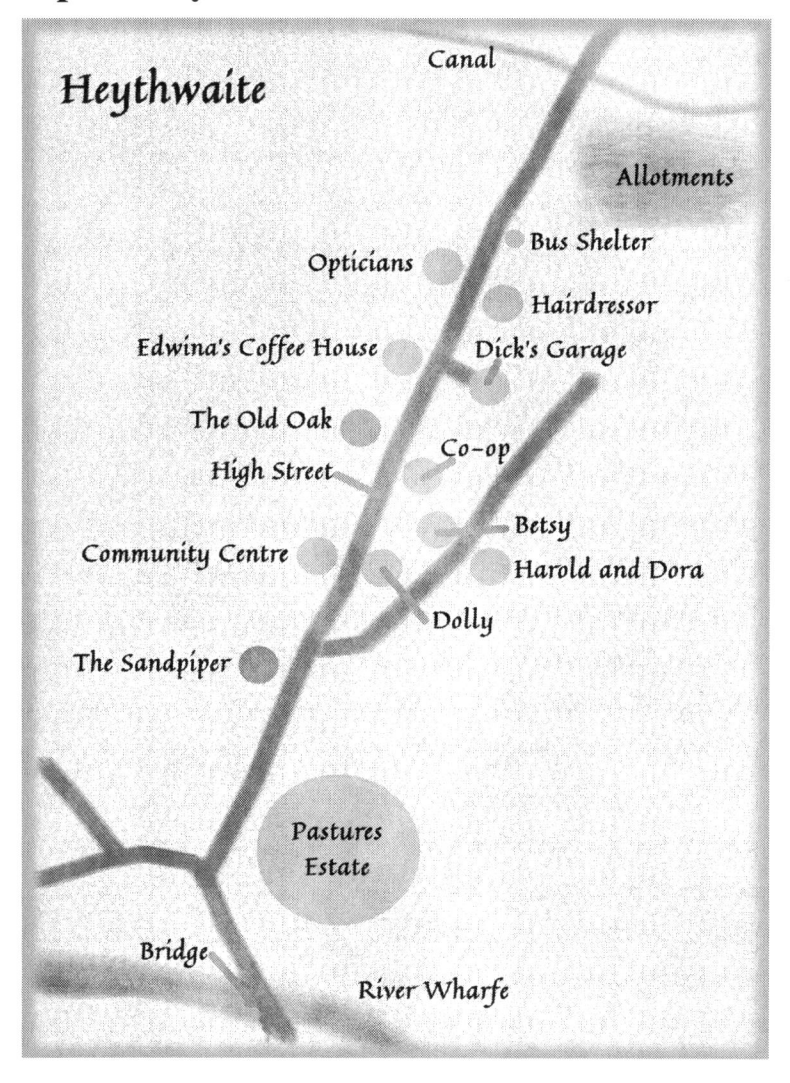

Heythwaite

Canal
Allotments
Bus Shelter
Opticians
Hairdresser
Edwina's Coffee House
Dick's Garage
The Old Oak
Co-op
High Street
Betsy
Community Centre
Harold and Dora
Dolly
The Sandpiper

Pastures Estate

Bridge
River Wharfe

Chapter 1 – Winter to Spring

January

It was mild for January and two elderly women were walking up the hill of the High Street of Heythwaite, a small town in the Yorkshire dales, nestled in a valley between three imposing hills, each of which rose above the tree line to reveal bracken moors, brown and barren in this season. "I see the shop's been sold," said the thin and scrawny Betsy, adjusting her headscarf as a gust of wind caught it.

"I think it's blowing up for a storm. More rain, just what we don't need," said Dolly, her friend of countless years, slightly younger, wearing loose fitting garments to hide her ample figure. "A coffee shop they say."

"We could do with one of those," said Betsy, her face deeply lined, never adorned with make-up and grey from the ten filter-less cigarettes she smoked daily, "A bakewell tart and a mug of tea in the morning. That'd set me up a treat."

Chalk and cheese was how people described Betsy and Dolly. Betsy was a straight speaking Yorkshire lass, into her seventies and her hair had not been coiffured for years, rarely experiencing shampoo either. Dolly contrasted, having a permanent wave of a style popular in the fifties, and face plastered with a thick layer of greasepaint.

"I hear that she's from Lancashire," said Dolly, also from Yorkshire, who held her tongue better than Betsy did, could be as direct as her friend, but without the rancour.

Chapter 1 – Winter to Spring

"Really, can't see that going down well round here," said Betsy, "Look, is that young Daniel."

Betsy waved and the young man returned the gesture as he sauntered over to the two pensioners. "Mornin' Mrs Longbottom, bit breezy isn't it?"

"It is, but warm for January. How's that apprenticeship going, lad?" said Dolly but didn't stop for Daniel to reply, "Your mother told me you're doing well. What's it you're going to be, an electrician, I think she said?"

"That's right, Mrs Jackson, a sparky. It's going fine, be finished later this year. Then I've got to find a job."

"You shouldn't have any problem, not with a trade like that, something worth doing, if you ask me," said Betsy.

"Did you hear about the break-in, Dick's garage?" said Daniel.

"No," said Betsy, "What did they take?"

"That's the surprising thing, they just ransacked the place, took nothing," said Daniel, "Luke, Dick's apprentice, told me. It was a mess by all accounts." There was the sound of a horn and Daniel glanced over at the green and grey van that had stopped by the road side. The lettering on the side indicated 'Yorkshire's Premier Electrical Contractor' and Daniel raised his hand at the driver. "Got to go. Nice talking to you ladies and have a good day."

Betsy and Dolly watched the youth leap into the van before its tyres screeched and it was gone, only the sound of its engine betraying the route it was taking towards the bigger towns.

Chapter 1 – Winter to Spring

"That sounds like a rum do," said Betsy, "Dick'll be mad at what they've done to his garage. I wonder what that was about?"

~

The weather had changed, now typical for January, a crisp frosty day. It found Betsy, who wanted bread and a pint of milk, walking briskly towards the shop. She noticed Dick at the entrance to his garage and changed direction to make a beeline for him. Dick spotted her but it was too late for him to duck inside, fearful that she would want something-for-nowt, as Yorkshire folk say. Dick was short, in his late fifties, thinning grey hair plastered to his head, slightly overweight and with a paunch from his fondness for Yorkshire ale.

"What's this I hear," said Betsy as she drew near.

"About the break-in?" said Dick, "Odd, they took nothing, just wrecked the place."

"What have the police done?" said Betsy.

"Forensics have been in. They've taken statements and the like but, so far, drawn a blank."

"This isn't right for round here," said Betsy, "We don't get trouble."

"No, it's peculiar," said Dick.

"Do you know what they wanted?" said Betsy.

"The police asked me the same thing. I haven't a clue," said Dick.

"What about Luke, does he know? Where is he anyway?"

Chapter 1 – Winter to Spring

"He's at college, he goes one day a week," said Dick, "The police interviewed him too, but he knew nothing."

"Funny business, but I've got to go. Dolly's coming round to mine and I need some milk for the brew."

"Well, I'll bid you a good day," said Dick, "These cars won't fix themselves."

"Indeed they won't," said Betsy, scuttling away.

~

"It's happened again," said Dolly as Betsy entered through her side door.

"What has?" said Betsy.

Dolly showed her friend into her front parlour where there were two chairs and a sofa decorated in complementing, but not identical, floral patterns. In the centre of the room was a small table adorned with a cream lace cloth. On it were plates embellished with scones, butter and a small pot of jam. Dolly pointed to a chair as she said, "I'll just fetch the tea and then I'll tell you."

Betsy chose the closest armchair as she knew it was firmer and waited. A few minutes later Dolly appeared, carrying a tray, upon which were two fine china cups with saucers, a tea pot, plates and knives for the scones. "This all looks nice," said Betsy, "Better than you get at mine."

Dolly smiled as she placed the tray on the table and planted her rear on the other armchair as she said, "I'll let it mash for a moment."

Chapter 1 – Winter to Spring

"So, tell me," said Betsy.

"Another break-in and, again, nothing taken," said Dolly.

"Where this time?" said Betsy, leaning forward in her chair.

"The small industrial estate, just behind what used to be the post office, before it closed," said Dolly.

"Are any of those units in use?" said Betsy.

"A couple," said Dolly, "It's the one that's a warehouse for that logistics company."

"What's a logistics company?" said Betsy.

"Who knows, dear?" said Dolly and she smiled, "Anyhow, it's like Dick's garage. They made a mess but didn't take anything."

"They're searching for something," said Betsy, "I wonder what?"

"Now that is an interesting question," said Dolly as she poured the tea.

~

Betsy and Dolly were outside the shop that was being refurbished. Two workmen were inside and one was heading for the door, holding a drill. As he passed the ladies, he greeted them and his accent was foreign, not from south of Yorkshire, but even further, possibly Poland. Betsy glanced at Dolly and nodded, knowingly, as she said, "It looks like you'll soon be finished. You're not from round here, are you lad?"

"Lad?" said the workman, his timbre unmistakably East European, "I haven't been called that for a while. A few more

Chapter 1 – Winter to Spring

weeks, I would think. I am from Southern Poland, near Kraków."

"Is it nice there, love?" said Dolly.

"Not as nice as Yorkshire. My name is Alojzy but people here call me Alex."

"Pleased to meet you, I'm sure," said Betsy, "but we need to be going, and you have work to do."

Alex smiled and bowed slightly as he said, "I do. Maybe I'll see you around?"

Betsy glanced at the workman and darted away leaving Dolly to say goodbye to Alex before she walked rapidly in Betsy's direction. Within a minute she'd caught up with her friend who had reached the bus stop, their destination, for they were catching the early bus into Skipton for the Wednesday market. "You think they might be involved?" said Betsy.

"Involved? In what? You don't mean the robberies?" said Dolly.

"They're not from round here and, anyway, robberies they weren't. Nothing was taken," said Betsy.

"You shouldn't judge people like that, just because they're not English," said Dolly, "It's the papers you read, they're brainwashing you."

"Not English!" said Betsy, chuckling, "No, it's not that. They're not from Yorkshire and that's enough for me."

~

Chapter 1 – Winter to Spring

Dick beckoned to Betsy as she was walking towards the Co-operative store. She turned up the short road to the garage, a cul-de-sac with Dick's business the only building in the street, and stopped in front of him. "Have you heard," said Dick, conspiratorially.

"Yes, and in broad daylight this time. Dolly was furious, it was her day for a haircut, shampoo and set. Waste of money if you ask me," said Betsy.

"Same thing, nothing removed, they just ransacked the place," said Dick, "What do you think it's all about?"

"Nobody saw a thing. Madge is distraught," said Betsy, "Poor lass, cried her eyes out when she saw the chaos."

Madge was the owner of the hairdresser that had been the target of the attack; she employed two stylists for the younger residents of the small town but tended to perform her magic on the older women herself. She was in her fifties, a similar age to Dick, and showed no sign of retiring any time soon. "She'll have been insured, like me, and they've been fine about it," said Dick, "Sent someone to help with the clean-up."

"That's a blessing, but it's worrying nevertheless," said Betsy, "It'd be nice to get to the bottom of it."

"Funny," said Dick and he stopped.

"What's funny?" said Betsy.

"Oh, nothing, just musing," said Dick. Betsy stared at the garage owner, tilted her head to one side but said nothing. The silence was deafening and Dick felt compelled to fill it. "Madge, George and me."

Chapter 1 – Winter to Spring

"George, who's that?" said Betsy.

"The fellow that owns the warehouse business, you know, they were done before Madge's place."

"Go on," said Betsy.

"Well, we were on that trip together, plus Alastair, the farmer, and his wife," said Dick.

"I remember, gallivanting around the Med, weren't you?" said Betsy.

"That's right, a cruise," said Dick.

"Alastair, lost his wife soon after he returned," said Betsy.

"Yes, tragic," said Dick, "Cancer, she had it while they were away. That's why they went."

"Five of you, on this cruise?" said Betsy, "Do you think Alistair could be next?"

"I'm jumping to conclusions," said Dick, "A coincidence, perhaps?"

"Anything strange happen on the trip?" said Betsy.

"Not that I can remember," said Dick.

"Maybe you should get your thinking cap on," said Betsy, turning to leave.

Dick scratched his forehead and watched as Betsy walked away. She stopped, turning to face him again. "I'd mention it to the police, just in case."

Dick nodded as Betsy scuttled off down to the main street.

~

13

Chapter 1 – Winter to Spring

"Three in one day," said Dolly, "I'm scared to leave the house." They were seated in Betsy's kitchenette, as she preferred to call it, being tiny. A small table, where Betsy ate most of her meals, was pushed against the wall. Dolly was squeezed into the narrower end while Betsy occupied the longer side. They were drinking tea from white mugs and each had a plate of toasted teacakes. "Did you make these?" said Dolly, pointing to the contents of the plate as she deviated from her topic of conversation.

"You know that I don't bake any more. There's no point, only me here. They're from the Co-op," said Betsy.

Dolly smiled, then continued, "Alistair's farm was attacked first, then Madge's home and now Dick's house. All within a few hours, and during the day. It's bad, Betsy."

"What about George?" said Betsy, remembering what Dick had said.

"Who is George, dear?" said Dolly.

"The warehouse, one of the industrial units, he owns it," said Betsy.

"I see, his business was raided too, you're looking for a pattern," said Dolly, "I don't think he lives here, he's from Skipton. That's what I heard."

Betsy slurped her tea and then informed Dolly about her conversation with Dick. Dolly listened without interrupting, nodding as she absorbed what she was hearing. "What do you make of that?" said Betsy finishing with a flourish.

"I'm not sure, at the moment," said Dolly.

Chapter 1 – Winter to Spring

~

"Nothing, nothing at all," said Madge. Dick was helping Madge clear up after the latest incident and Dolly had arrived to help. Madge was distressed as she moved through the clutter, idly picking up pieces and putting them down anywhere.

"Is it alright for us to do this?" said Dick, "The police have been?"

"Yes, and the insurance company, again." said Madge.

"Why do you keep asking me about the cruise?" said Madge to Dolly.

"Something that Dick told Betsy," said Dolly and she turned to Dick, saying, "You have mentioned this to the police, haven't you?"

Dick nodded as he said, "They just took a note of it but, with George's place in Skipton looted, they should take it more seriously. Again, nothing taken, that seems to be the pattern."

"Only those on the jaunt seem to have been hit," said Dolly, "Doesn't that seem odd? You can't think of anything out of the ordinary that happened?"

"No, we had a good time that's all," said Dick, "Bought a few trinkets in the ports that we visited, junk mostly, but otherwise we enjoyed the sun and the booze."

"Alistair, he had a row with someone who tried to take his wife's handbag," said Madge.

"Ran after him, and Catherine was worried," said Dick, "She had cancer, you know?"

Chapter 1 – Winter to Spring

"Yes, thank you," said Dolly and she turned to Betsy, whispering, "Lancashire, they're not like us."

"Surely, they are not."

~

Dolly was at her friend's again in her kitchenette, Betsy smiling a toothless grin. With a grubby cloth, Betsy cleaned the surface of the table, decked with a plastic coated tablecloth, brushing crumbs onto the floor. "Where are your dentures, Betsy?"

"I don't need them when it's just you and me," said Betsy, chortling.

"I've been thinking about these break-ins," said Dolly.

"They've stopped. The police don't seem to have arrested anyone," said Betsy.

"Dick told me that nothing exceptional happened on their cruise, except …"

"Except?" repeated Betsy.

"He mentioned that Alastair's wife's handbag had been filched."

"What do you expect in those foreign parts," said Betsy, "Beggars and thieves, all of them."

Dolly shook her head and looked to the ceiling. "No, Alastair chased the man who took it, even though Catherine told him not to."

"Did he?" said Betsy.

Chapter 1 – Winter to Spring

"Clouted the chap, Dick told me, and then Alastair recovered the bag."

"Empty, I suppose?" said Betsy.

"That's the odd thing, nothing had been removed, but Alastair told Dick that the handbag hadn't contained anything valuable," said Dolly, "Catherine had her purse and money on her."

"Sensible, if you ask me. Why did he go to the trouble of running after the thief? He put himself at risk, especially in foreign parts. The police there aren't like ours."

"I think I'm going to talk to Alastair," said Dolly.

"Are you sure? Better to let sleeping dogs lie." said Betsy.

~

Alastair's farmhouse was on the outskirts of the village and Robert helped run the farm with Alastair since Catherine's death. Robert was Alastair's son and was married to Amy who was expecting a baby at the end of the winter. Alastair was walking in the fields with Bouncer, a border collie, full of energy but well trained by the farmer. He was heading for his flock of curly fleeced Wensleydale sheep when he saw the pensioners. He yelled, waving his arm, calling Bouncer to heel, as he spotted Dolly and Betsy plodding towards him. "It's good to see you," he said, as they came closer, "What brings you up here?"

"Oh, wanted to see how you are after that unfortunate incident," said Dolly.

Chapter 1 – Winter to Spring

"The break in? I wasn't the only one to suffer and it looks like it's finished," said Alastair, Bouncer now waiting patiently by his side, "They made a mess and I was worried about Amy. She's expecting you know?"

"How is she, doing fine I hope, when is it due?" said Betsy.

"End of March, all being well," said Alastair, "She's a tough Yorkshire lass, she'll not let anything ruffle her, that one. I'm off to see the Wensleydale's. You can come with me or, if you like, Amy's in the kitchen and she'll make you a cuppa. I won't be long and I can join you there."

"A brew sounds nice," said Dolly, not wishing to walk any further up the muddy field, made worse by the incessant winter rains.

"Ten minutes I should be, tops," said Alastair as he continued his walk, telling the collie to follow him.

Dolly and Betsy wandered down the grassland to the gate, avoiding the gelatinous sludge littering the ground between the gate posts. Betsy opened the farmhouse door tentatively and shouted a greeting. When she heard nothing she repeated it but louder this time. A door at the far end of the yard opened and a head popped out and said, "I'm in the kitchen, over here. Watch out for the mud and worse. How about a mug of tea?"

Dolly picked her way hesitantly across the farmyard while Betsy, in her Wellington boots, strode confidently towards Amy. As she reached the door, she removed the wellies and stepped inside in her stocking feet. Dolly arrived later, stopped at the door and climbed onto the second step, removing her

Chapter 1 – Winter to Spring

sodden shoes, before entering the kitchen. "My, my, it's mucky out there."

"Farms," said Amy, needing no further explanation. She placed tea leaves into a teapot, took a massive black kettle from the Aga range and poured boiling water over Harrogate's finest blend of Betty's tea. She took three large mugs from a cupboard, the outside well fingered from years of use, poured milk into each cup, fresh from the cow that morning, as she said, "You want white, yes?"

Both Dolly and Betsy nodded as Amy came to join them at the large pine table in the centre of a classic farmhouse kitchen. "Best let it brew. Is dad joining us?"

"Ten minutes he said, love," said Dolly.

"That probably means twenty," said Amy, "I'll make his fresh when he's here. I've some oatmeal biscuits, baked this morning. Interested?"

"Never say no to a biscuit," said Betsy.

A couple of minutes passed and Amy walked over to the cupboard to retrieve the cookie jar and pour the tea. She brought one cup and the biscuits over and then went back for the remaining mugs. "What brings you to the farm? We don't have many visitors."

"It's a bit of a trek at our age," said Betsy.

Amy smiled and waited for one of the pensioners to enlighten her. "It's about the break-in," said Dolly, "We wanted to check that you were alright."

"That's nice of you but, yes, we are doing just fine," said Amy, "It was a bit of a shock but others fared worse. We had to suffer it once, some weren't so lucky."

"No, their businesses and homes were both struck," said Dolly, "Madge still isn't over it."

"Isn't she?" said Amy, "I must go and see her. I need my hair done too. There seems little point in having it styled since I've been here."

"Waste of money," said Betsy.

"Oh, take no notice of her. It's nice to be pampered once in a while. A girl needs that," said Dolly.

A smile spread across Amy's face as she said, "You are right, I'll make the effort."

"You know what's odd, about these break-ins, I mean," said Betsy.

"The cruise, we'd worked it out too," said Amy, "Only those who were on that trip have been targeted."

"We think they're looking for something," said Dolly, "Something of value."

"I can't think what. Dad certainly hasn't anything of value."

"Only you and Robert," said Alastair, entering through the outer door, "And the little one due soon, of course."

"Anyhow, it's been a year since the trip," said Amy, "Why now?"

Chapter 1 – Winter to Spring

"A good question and we went for the experience, our last chance of a little happiness," said Alistair, walking over to join them.

Amy put her hand on Alastair's arm as she said, "So, you see, we don't know why any of this is happening but we're glad it's stopped."

"For now," said Betsy.

"Why do you say that?" said Alastair.

"The police don't seem to know what's happened. Who's to say they won't return?"

"Security's a bit tighter here now, they'd find it harder than they did before," said Amy, "The insurance company insisted."

"It's a mystery, one that'll probably never be solved," said Dolly. Alastair nodded as Amy pondered, a look of puzzlement on her face. Dolly glanced at Betsy and they both knew that something was amiss.

~

Amy was on the settee, her head resting against Robert's shoulder. Alastair had settled in his favourite armchair, newspaper resting on his lap, ready to read later. "Asked about the break-in, did they?" said Robert.

"They were concerned, for me mostly," said Amy, smiling and patting her expanding abdomen, "Especially with little Jethro arriving this year."

Robert and Amy had decided not to ask their midwife about the sex of their baby, preferring a surprise when the time arrived. Alastair had told them that they shouldn't use 'it' to describe their bump and he'd started calling it Jethro and the name stuck. "That Betsy, she's a busybody," said Robert.

"Oh, she's not that bad, and Dolly's a dear," said Amy.

"You any idea at all, dad?" said Robert. Alastair gazed into the distance and Amy peered at her husband.

"What is it?" said Amy.

"Oh, nothing," said Alastair and he picked up his newspaper. Robert shook his head gently towards Amy. His gaze articulated the unspoken words 'all in good time'.

February

Betsy donned her Wellington boots, wrapped a woollen muffler around her, added a gilet and trench coat before covering her head with a headscarf and wrapping her hands in fur lined mittens. She opened the front door of her terraced house, in a road that joined the High Street, and stepped down the two Yorkshire stone steps onto a walkway layered white, for winter was reminding Betsy of its capabilities. Across the road, Harold, a neighbour, was clearing snow from the path outside of his house and he waved at Betsy. "Bit raw," Betsy shouted as she gingerly traipsed down to the High Street, towards Dolly's house near the bottom of the hill.

"You be careful, now, it's treacherous," shouted Harold.

"I will, and if everyone cleared their pavement like you, it would be easier for me."

Chapter 1 – Winter to Spring

Harold smiled as he shouted back, "Can't wait for spring. I can get back to the allotment then."

Betsy lifted her head as she replied, "Days are getting longer. Won't be long now. We're heading in the right direction." Trudging slowly down the lane, Betsy turned right at the end of her road and walked along High Street until she reached Dolly's home. It was a two story terraced house with a tiny front garden, bounded by a black wrought iron fence finished in a spear-head design. Betsy pulled on the squeaky gate as Dolly opened the front door. "It's bitter out there," she said, "Come on in and warm yourself. The kettle's on."

Inside, Betsy removed her layers and boots, depositing them in the hall. Dolly placed Betsy's coat, scarf and gloves carefully on the hooks of her 1950's-style hall coat-rack and stand. The wellies, she placed upside down on strong wooden pegs, designed for the purpose. "Go through to the kitchen, we're in there today," said Dolly, "Scones are nearly cooked."

Betsy, now in her stocking feet, walked past the parlour with its bay window facing the high street, along the hallway and into the kitchen overlooking a paved yard. Dolly and her late husband had combined the dining room and kitchen some years previously and had added a small conservatory that Dolly used only in warmer weather. "Nice and cosy in here," said Betsy as she plonked herself down at the square pine table in the centre of the room.

"Was the path slippy?" said Dolly.

"Just my road," said Betsy, "They've salted the main routes. Harold was clearing his pathway."

Chapter 1 – Winter to Spring

"He's a nice man," said Dolly,

"Pity about Dora," said Betsy, grinning toothlessly.

Dora was Harold's long standing wife, a stoic Yorkshire woman who suffered fools, and many others, not at all. "That's why he spends so much time at the allotment with Walter and Bert, dear," said Dolly, smiling. Dolly took two fine china cups, decorated with a floral pattern, the rim edged in gold, plus two matching saucers and placed them gently on the table. She added corresponding plates and then placed tea leaves in a Royal Doulton Minerva teapot and topped it up with scalding water. "I'll let it brew," said Dolly as she walked over to the oven, pulled down the windowed door, and removed a tray of golden coloured scones, beautifully risen.

"My, they look nice," said Betsy, salivating in anticipation.

Dolly put the scone tray on her counter side, using a trivet to protect the surface, placed four of the pastries on a larger plate and put it on the table, next to jam and butter. "I opened the apricot yesterday, I know it's your favourite."

"It is," said Betsy, leaning forward to pour the tea.

"Leave the scones for a few minutes to cool. Then, they won't crumble." The scones devoured and commencing their third cup of tea, Dolly said, "That funny business, there's been no repeat."

"Odd, and the police haven't discovered anything either," said Betsy.

"What do you reckon?"

Chapter 1 – Winter to Spring

"Not sure," said Betsy, "Dick says we should be grateful that it's over."

"Might be good advice," said Dolly.

Betsy glanced over at her friend and twisted her face, her head dipping to the right as she said, "You're not certain are you?"

"Seems peculiar. Something happened on that cruise and I think Alastair knows what it was. He had a shifty look and I think Amy might be in the dark."

"What about Robert?" said Betsy.

"I don't know but, the way those two are, if Amy doesn't know, you can bet your bottom dollar that Robert is clueless too."

Betsy lifted her cup to her mouth, slurping noisily and, as she finished the dregs, said, "Not much point in approaching Alastair again, but ..."

"Amy," said Dolly, interrupting, "Is that what you are thinking?"

"Yes, exactly. If anyone can get to the bottom of this, she can."

"Especially in her current state," said Dolly.

"I don't think she'll use her pregnancy. Sympathy isn't her style, I'd say."

"Just like you, Betsy."

~

Chapter 1 – Winter to Spring

Tuesday was Dolly's pamper day when she visited Madge for a shampoo and set; sometimes she added a blue rinse, but not today. The door chimed as she entered and Madge looked up and smiled. "Take a seat, Dolly. I will be a few minutes, just finishing off."

Dolly picked up a magazine and opened a page as she heard the 'ding' of the door. She raised her head to witness Amy walking through the entrance. Dolly rose to her feet, greeted her with a hug as Amy seated herself next to Dolly. "I took your advice, I'm having my hair done," said Amy.

"Good for you, dear," said Dolly.

They spoke pleasantries for a few moments, Dolly asking about Robert, Alastair and the imminent arrival of their progeny and Amy enquiring about Betsy. The British obsession with the changeable weather was their next topic; the chill and snow had been replaced with milder but wetter weather. "No further incidents, thankfully," Dolly managed to inject into the conversation.

"The break-ins, you mean?"

"Yes, must have been quite frightening."

"We're fine. As I mentioned last time we met, security is tighter now," said Amy.

"Dick was telling me about what happened on the cruise," said Dolly.

"Oh, what happened?"

"The robbery, or should I say the attempted theft of Catherine's handbag," said Dolly.

Chapter 1 – Winter to Spring

"Tell me more," said Amy, her eyes wide with surprise.

"Didn't you know about it, dear? Someone grabbed Catherine's bag. Alastair pursued him and recovered it."

"He never said a word," said Amy.

"Ran after him, Dick told me. Gave him a bit of a beating by all accounts. Poor Catherine was distraught. She told him to leave it, worried about him, she was."

"Sounds like dad," said Amy, her gaze distant.

At that point, Madge called over to Dolly, as she was ready to start, and Dolly smiled at Amy as she stood, saying, "Pop in for a tea or coffee some time, love. Let me know and I'll bake a nice Victoria sponge."

"You're on," said Amy, nodding her head.

As Dolly took her seat in the pamper-chair, Amy picked up a magazine and flicked past a few pages, without reading them. Her mind was elsewhere, wondering why Alastair hadn't mentioned Catherine's handbag and, more to the point, why Catherine had kept it quiet when she was alive. She wondered if Robert knew about it.

~

Betsy was already in Dolly's lounge when the doorbell rang. "Can you get that," shouted Dolly, "It'll be Amy, she's right on time."

Betsy pushed herself up from the comfortable armchair, making her way down the hall to the front door. Amy stood on the doorstep, under the covered porch, sheltering from the wind

Chapter 1 – Winter to Spring

and rain. She was folding her umbrella when the door opened, revealing Betsy who stepped aside from the entrance, saying, "Get yourself in out of the rain."

Amy shook the umbrella outside before stepping through. She placed the brolly in the hall coat stand and removed her anorak and scarf, which she hung on one of the hooks. "Go through to the lounge," Dolly said, poking her head around the kitchen door, "Tea or coffee, love?"

"A cup of tea, please," said Amy.

Betsy showed Amy through to Dolly's lounge with its pretty bay window overlooking the High Street. It was furnished with a two-seater sofa, a firm lady-style and softer upright armchair. In the centre of the room was a coffee table adorned with fine china cups on saucers, paired plates, spoons and cake forks. Betsy lowered her posterior onto her preferred sturdy chair, suggesting that Amy take the settee. Dolly walked through the door carrying a tray with her best teapot, milk in a dainty jug, sugar in a china bowl and a well risen sponge cake filled with her home made strawberry jam. "Here let me take that," said Amy, standing, "It looks superb."

"It's all right, love, I can manage." Dolly placed the tray on a side table and transported its contents carefully to the coffee table. "The tea will take a couple of minutes. Are you well Amy, you are looking it? Pregnancy suits you, my dear."

"I'm feeling fine," said Amy, "No problems yet, touch wood."

Chapter 1 – Winter to Spring

"When are you due?" said Betsy, "Alistair said the end of March."

"Nearer the 20th, if the dates are right. The midwife thought that they're probably correct, from the scan."

"Not long, then," said Betsy.

"Sleeping is a challenge. I seem to spend more time in the toilet than slumbering."

"Oh, I remember that," said Dolly.

Betsy poured the tea as Dolly cut each of them a generous portion of Victoria sponge and silence prevailed whilst they ate. "That was wonderful," said Amy.

"More, dear?"

"I'll burst!"

"You look like you might anyway," said Betsy, grinning.

Amy picked up her cup, pushed herself back and leant into the settee as she said, "When we met at the hairdresser, Dolly."

"Waste of money!" said Betsy.

Dolly gave her friend a sideways look as she answered Amy, "Yes, dear."

"You mentioned that someone had tried to steal mum's handbag, when they went on the cruise."

"Catherine's, yes, can't remember where they were."

"They were in Mallorca. I asked dad about it; he hadn't wanted to worry us when they returned. He told me that mum's cancer was enough of a concern. That's why they'd kept quiet about the incident."

Chapter 1 – Winter to Spring

"Was it, dear?"

Amy glanced at Dolly and then at Betsy. They seemed to be expecting more. "That's all he mentioned. Why are you looking like that?"

"Oh, its nothing, dear," said Dolly, "I wondered if he might be able to shed some more light on the reason for the break-ins. Another tea, Amy?"

March

"Are you sure?" said Harold, "Worms, you say."

"I'm certain, I tell you. It's their secret. Eric heard them talking about a wormery," said Walter, pulling the pipe from his mouth and blowing smoke as he spoke. Walter's family had originated in Jamaica and he had the look of someone who was from the Caribbean. That's as far as it went; Walter was born in Yorkshire, had the accent to match and was staunchly proud of his birthright.

"Doesn't sound right to me," said Bert, "How does that work?"

The three septuagenarians were in a wooden shed at their shared council allotment. It was early March and still chilly but the sun was higher in the sky and there was warmth in it. The soil was too wet to work so they sat on rickety chairs around a paraffin stove, the smell of the oil vapours mixing with the fumes of Walter's pipe. They were discussing the Allotment Growers Championship to be held in July of that year. Competition was fierce and their Super Six team, six being the

Chapter 1 – Winter to Spring

number of their allotment, had triumphed, achieving all of the vegetable growing prizes for the previous ten years.

Except for last year.

They'd been usurped by newcomers, Ambrose and his wife Beatrice, both young, in their sixties, who had won the award for the longest carrots. Worse, they'd triumphed in their first growing season and, as Beatrice collected the cup, she'd peered straight at the Super Six and smiled in a triumphant manner. They'd had the audacity to name their team Victorious Thirty. Harold had watched Dora, his tubby wife, arms crossed, face stern, lips pursed and in her best frock, watch as the perfectly turned out Beatrice charmed the judges and walked jubilantly through the crowds, smiling sweetly, clutching the prize, while ensuring everyone could see it.

"What're you lads playing at?" Dora had said, "You're losing your touch, letting the likes of her win."

"We didn't take much notice of them last season, what with them being new around here," said Harold.

"We won't make that mistake again," said Walter.

"What about these worms?" said Bert.

"It's just a theory," said Walter, "What we need is proof."

Harold leaned forward in a conspiratorial manner and spoke, his voice a whisper, "Dora says they had a delivery the other day. A stroke of luck. The postman, he's new to the patch, asked her about the address. She said the package was labelled 'Fragile, Living Animals' and she looked up the company that

Chapter 1 – Winter to Spring

sent the package on that internet thing. She's a dab hand at that. Can't get on with it myself."

"What did she find?" said Walter.

"Speak up will you Harold. My hearing's not what it used to be," said Bert.

"Sorry," said Harold, continuing to whisper, "Apparently, they supply a mix of tiger worms and dendrobaena."

"Maybe he's a fisherman? Those dendrobaena are used as bait I think," said Bert.

"They were addressed to her, Beatrice, and I don't think she's an angler," said Harold.

"What does your Dora make of it?" said Bert.

"She's as mad as hell that they triumphed last year. She thinks Beatrice is stuck-up. Can't stand her. The pressure's on lads. We can't let them win again or my life won't be worth living," said Harold.

"Nor mine," said Bert, "Dora's been talking to my Elsie and she's been giving me grief."

Walter smiled at his friends' dilemma. He'd forsaken marriage and had settled into a comfortable routine in his dotage, happy with his lot in life. "Like I was telling you, maybe we should get some of those worms, as an insurance," said Walter.

"What do we do with them?" said Bert.

"Search me," said Harold.

"Then we need to find out," said Walter.

Chapter 1 – Winter to Spring

~

They'd drawn up a roster to guarantee that someone was at allotment six for the next week so that they could watch their rivals from the safety of the shed. Using binoculars, they had an excellent view of their competition on number thirty, close to the canal and opposite them, separated by two rows of allotments. The first morning was Harold's turn and it was uneventful. Bert was present for the afternoon and saw nothing. Walter took the evening shift and that was when Beatrice and Ambrose visited. The victorious allotment holders arrived at five o'clock and Ambrose was clasping a cardboard box. Walter watched through the binoculars as Beatrice made for the compost heap, resplendent in her sea blue Wellington boots, decorated with colourful flowers, and matching mackintosh. The mound was at the bottom end of the allotment and was surrounded by a tanalised wooden fence on three sides. She took a spade and dug out the centre of the pile to ground level. When she'd completed her task, Ambrose placed the box into the hole she'd made, without opening the container. Beatrice replaced the partly rotted compost over the box, then used a hose to water the mound for a few minutes before placing a tarpaulin over the heap. Finished, the pair worked on their plot, preparing it for the season to come.

~

"A box, did you say?" said Harold.

"Cardboard, about this size," said Walter opening out his hands to show the size of the box, a one foot cube.

"They didn't open it?" said Bert.

Chapter 1 – Winter to Spring

"No, I was puzzled by that," said Walter.

"Maybe they're hiding something in the mound?" said Harold.

"Why would they turn the hose on it?" said Walter, "The box would be sodden."

"Yes, it wouldn't take long to disintegrate," said Bert.

It was mid-morning and the three amigos were in their regular place, seated around the oil heater in their shed enjoying a cup of tea and a chocolate digestive. What Walter had discovered was baffling but it was what they should do about his findings that was taxing them. Elsie, Bert's wife, and egged on by Dora, had been pestering Bert. She wanted no outsiders winning the competition this year. "Well, there's only one way to find out," said Harold.

"What are you suggesting, Harold?" said Bert.

"When do they usually come over to the allotment, Walter?" said Harold.

"Your Dora said they like to have their tea at five so they do a couple of hours before that. If we said two, we'd be on the safe side," said Walter and he winked at Harold. Dora knew much of what happened in Heythwaite, little escaped her.

"Are you ..." said Bert but he didn't finish as Harold took up the slack.

"Pass me that spade, if you would Bert, we're going to see what's in that box." Bert was to act as look-out, to whistle loudly if he saw Ambrose or Beatrice and then keep them talking. Nonchalantly, Walter and Harold made for the canal,

Chapter 1 – Winter to Spring

their cover should the worse happen. The impression they wanted to give was that they were strolling down the tow path. They arrived at allotment thirty and looked around, glancing at Bert who gave a thumbs up sign. Harold, bent over double, moved towards the compost heap, spade in hand and knelt as he reached the mound, hoping that the fence would conceal him. Tentatively, he removed the tarpaulin, a few layers of compost, then more before he glanced in the hole. The top of the box was visible and so were the hundreds of worms that were escaping into the heap. 'Bingo', thought Walter as he refilled the hole, put the canvas back in place and they made their escape.

~

"Bang on time, you say," said Dolly.

"She's back home now. Robert was more stressed than Amy, by all accounts," said Betsy.

They were sauntering up the high street towards the bus stop where they were to catch the seventy-one service to Skipton for their weekly outing to the market. The air was still cool, but the season was changing and the sun becoming warmer. The snowdrops were finished but daffodils had started to decorate the gardens and verges, radiating cheery colour to bid farewell to the winter. Spring was on it's way, Dolly's favourite time of year. She anticipated it by bedecking her house with decorous cut flowers and potted hyacinths, their scent permeating every room. Betsy was indifferent to the seasons but welcomed the lengthening days and the promise this offered. "Robert will be

Chapter 1 – Winter to Spring

pleased. A boy to help on the farm. What have they called him?" said Dolly.

"They haven't yet," said Betsy, "They seemed to think it'd be a girl and were going to call her after Catherine."

"I thought they didn't know the sex?"

"Oh, they didn't. Got it into their head, that's all," said Betsy.

"I'm sure they'll choose a name soon," said Dolly.

The two old friends arrived at the bus stop and Betsy glanced at her watch. They had a few minutes to wait so they sat on a bench, against the wall, in the sun. "I was talking to Harold, the other day," said Betsy.

"Oh, yes," said Dolly, "How is he?"

"Him and Dora are fine and he's spending time down the allotment again."

"Still a bit early for that, I would have thought," said Dolly.

"You know what they are like. Get old blokes together and they can talk the hind legs off a donkey."

Dolly smiled as she remembered the Allotment Growers Championship at the flower and produce show of the previous year. "They weren't very happy when the newcomers walked off with that prize. Dora's face was like thunder."

"Harold looked shifty when I mentioned it. They're up to something. Could be interesting this year."

As Dolly turned her head, smiling, she spotted the bus turn the corner at the top of the hill and she beckoned to Betsy who was already on her feet with her arm outstretched, requesting

Chapter 1 – Winter to Spring

the bus to stop. As the bus came close, the bus driver waved and grinned at Betsy as he screeched to a halt. The doors slid open and Betsy stepped forward. "In a hurry, are you Hamid?"

"Hello Mrs Longbottom and I see you have that nice Mrs Jackson with you. Free ride to Skipton is it?"

"Less of your cheek, young man," said Betsy, placing her bus-pass on the receptor. Dolly followed, asking the driver about his family, and then walked up the bus to join Betsy, who was seated by the window. Once he was certain that the ladies were comfortable, the driver accelerated slowly down the street towards the market town of Skipton.

~

By the end of March the sun was higher in the sky and the day length exceeded that of the night. The air was cool but the winter rains were behind. The soil was better and some of the tougher seeds had been sown on the allotment, particularly broad beans and onion sets. Potato tubers were planted but they needed constant attention to avoid being nipped by a late frost. Walter and Harold were preparing their seed beds when Bert arrived clutching a large box. Inside it was a smaller one marked 'Living Animals – Handle with Care'. The day of the worms had arrived. Elsie, Bert's wife, had purchased the worms online from a Yorkshire supplier recommended by the prestigious Royal Horticultural Society. On their web site was a formidable set of instructions with dire warnings of what could go awry if they were not followed. Elsie had printed the guidance and Bert had folded it into his anorak pocket. Bert wandered into the shed as Walter and Harold broke off from

Chapter 1 – Winter to Spring

their toil to join him. He placed the box on a shelf by the window and retrieved the print-out from his jacket. He was reading it as his compatriots arrived. "Can't make head, nor tail of this," said Bert, shaking his head.

"You've got the worms, then," said Harold.

"Here, you have a look at this," said Bert, passing the instructions to Walter.

Walter took the leaflet from Bert and scanned its contents, mumbling as he read. Finally he said, "Looks complicated and it says here the worms are a bit sensitive."

"It can't be that difficult. Ambrose and Beatrice managed, even with her in those blue wellies!" said Harold.

"We've got to remove the worms before we spread the compost, after they've done their work. That's what it says," said Bert.

"Stuff that for a game of soldiers," said Walter.

"Are you sure about this, Walter?" said Bert.

Walter was wavering, especially when he read that twelve months was needed for the worms to do their work. Then he spotted his escape route. Worms produced a liquid fertiliser and they didn't have to wait a year for that. "What worms do we have, Bert," said Walter, deflecting the conversation to give him time to think.

Bert put his hand in his left jacket pocket and retrieved a crumpled piece of paper that he unfolded. Stumbling over the words, he read from the invoice, "Eisenia foetida, Eisenia andreii and Dendrabaena veneta, it say here."

Chapter 1 – Winter to Spring

"Means nothing to me," said Harold as Walter nodded his head.

"We've got to change the way we compost, capture the liquid that the worms make. We'll be able to make use of it this season, and the compost next. It's rich in nitrogen and potassium, like a tomato feed."

"Why don't we just buy that?" said Bert, puzzled, worrying that they'd bought a pup.

Walter, who's feet were definitely chilling, retorted in desperation, "Look, do you want to beat Ambrose and his stuck-up wife, or not?"

~

"Coffee, dear," said Beatrice as she placed two white china cups, embellished with bright red poppies, onto coasters depicting scenes around the Yorkshire countryside. These had been placed on a sparkling glass topped coffee table, supported by stone statues of Swaledale sheep. Ambrose sat in their heated Orangery, half way down the spacious and well presented garden, flicking through his daily newspaper, The Telegraph. Beatrice had prepared the coffee at their built-in espresso machine in the centre of the single room.

"Thank you, love," said Ambrose with a strong Yorkshire accent that belied his name, appearance and surroundings.

Beatrice, hair perfectly coiffured, as always, wore a designer blouse, tight fitting stretch-jeans and comfortable black leather shoes. Her neck was adorned with a silk scarf, wrists bedecked with gold bracelets and her ring finger sported a huge diamond and wide platinum band. They had a large house in the exclusive 'Pastures' estate in a cul-de-sac off the bottom of the high street, near the River Wharfe. Ambrose's business had been a successful one but he'd been forced to retire after a heart attack, culminating in open heart bypass surgery and a period of convalescence. Although fully recovered, he'd decided that 'life was for living' and felt that he'd earned enough to give him and Beatrice a comfortable retirement. The health shock had focussed his mind but it hadn't damped his competitive spirit. Beatrice loved her garden and she'd planned it to comprise several 'rooms', one formal, near the house, where the Orangery had been built, one with a pond and flowing water and finally, a wild area furthest from their home, with a selection of recently planted trees and a meadow of grasses and wild English flowers. Within this area were the bee-hives and Beatrice was becoming a competent beekeeper, taking a British Beekeepers' Association course. To complement her garden, Beatrice had wanted to cultivate organically grown vegetables to provide fresh produce for the strict diet that she'd enforced for Ambrose. A vegetable plot didn't fit into her garden design and, when an allotment came free, she was quick to act, contacting the Allotment Growers Association immediately. Charming and forceful, Beatrice met little resistance from officialdom; she and Ambrose took on the tenancy in time for the growing season, their first year in Heythwaite. Winning a prize at the championship competition had been the cherry on the bakewell tart. They grew the longest carrots that year, to the annoyance of the incumbents; she was determined to repeat the feat in the coming season and take

Chapter 1 – Winter to Spring

more prizes. She had a trick up her sleeve for super-sized carrots, turnips, onions, leeks and cabbages. This year, she planned to take all of the prizes; there would be no stopping her. Ambrose knew better than to interfere.

~

"Will you have another cup, dear?" said Dolly as she poured boiling water from a large kettle over tea leaves in a well used tea pot, "I see you haven't touched the last one."

Amy smiled, looked towards Dolly and nodded. Betsy and Dolly were visiting Amy and her new addition who was now gently sucking at his mummy's breast. The homely place was strewn with the paraphernalia of a baby: pram, changing mat, basket of nappies, the kit and ointments needed for that job and a clothes horse full of tiny attire, airing. "I seem to have no time for myself. This little one demands all of my attention," said Amy.

"It'll get easier," said Dolly, walking over to Amy and clearing away two cups of partially consumed tea.

"The lads are having to fend for themselves," said Amy.

"It'll do them no harm," said Betsy.

"How's Robert coping?" said Dolly.

"You know," said Amy, "I thought he was going to be a great dad, but he's surprised even me. He has the farm to run but makes it over to the house as much as possible, finding excuses to pass this way. He's attentive, besotted even, changes the nappies and is always home for bath time. It's become his job."

Chapter 1 – Winter to Spring

"You're lucky, my lass," said Dolly, "It wasn't like that in my day."

"Alastair is over the moon," said Amy, and then lowered her voice, "There were floods of tears when he first saw Jethro."

"After all that's happened, it's probably relief. Have you chosen the name Jethro?" said Betsy. Amy chuckled as she explained that Jethro was the name they'd given to her bump, as a holding pattern, until they decided on a final name. Robert and she had discussed it liberally but hadn't found one that they both liked, so Jethro it was, for the moment. Amy finished feeding and, supporting the baby's head, started tapping him lightly on his back, to free trapped wind. Dolly placed Amy's fresh tea on a table, beside her armchair, and leaned forward. Amy understood the gesture and passed Jethro to Dolly who cradled the infant in her arms and continued what Amy had commenced. Gratefully, Amy sipped the tea as Dolly took a seat in a high backed chair, by the table. Glad of some respite, Amy gazed over at Dolly as she handled Amy's precious bundle, the years since Dolly did the same to her own peeling away, old competences returning.

"You asked me about the break-in, a while back," said Amy.

"Yes, dear," said Dolly.

"Alistair's tongue has loosened lately," said Amy.

"Must be this little one," said Betsy.

Amy smiled and her gaze moved to Betsy as she said, "Alastair was angry when he caught up with the thief. He

Chapter 1 – Winter to Spring

snatched back Catherine's bag but he also ripped a 'man bag' off the guy's shoulder."

Betsy looked puzzled and Dolly explained, "Young men carry them now, dear, especially on the continent."

"Anyhow, Alastair took it back to the boat and threw the bag into the Mediterranean, once they'd left port."

"Any idea what was in it?" said Betsy.

"Alastair told me that he didn't take much notice, just wanted to give the thief some of his own medicine."

"Whatever it was, looks like it was important, for them to come searching for it," said Dolly.

"Well, we'll not find out now, it's in Davy Jones locker," said Betsy, glancing at Dolly.

~

Walter had worked most of the morning on his project; if he never saw worms again it would be too soon. He'd moved the compost heap, spreading the best rotted on their plot. Then, he'd restructured the base of the heap, giving it a sloping gradient, raising it from the ground, sufficient so that any run-off could be captured in a tray now positioned for the purpose. He'd returned half of the semi-rotted material and placed the box of mixed species worms at its centre. He'd completed adding the rest of the compost when Bert arrived. "Wondered where you were. You should have waited for me."

"You're just in time," said Walter, "Give it some water, will you, and then you can help me with the tarpaulin. It needs covering, apparently." Walter explained what he'd done to Bert

Chapter 1 – Winter to Spring

who nodded. He wasn't convinced that all of Walter's hard work was worth the effort, but didn't wish to burst Walter's bubble. Bert glanced at the tray, started to mouth a question about what happened to it when it rained, or the wind blew, but held his counsel. He knew that Walter was like a ferret, he'd keep going until out of energy or his prey was caught. Bert decided to deflect the conversation and asked about the whereabouts of the missing gardener, Harold.

"They're visiting Dora's sister, in Harrogate."

"She must have some brass to live there," said Bert, repeating what he often remarked.

"Oh, they don't live in the centre, not sure where, near the railway line to Leeds, I think. Reckon he'll be away all day."

"Is that the sister who bakes?" said Bert.

Walter smiled, "Aye, lad, you're right. Might be in for a treat tomorrow."

~

Ambrose and Beatrice were at their allotment, number thirty, near the canal. The early seeds were planted in regimented lines across the plot, the distance between them measured with precision and identified by strings held taught between markers, labelled in indelible ink with the crop name. Broad beans, beetroot, parsnip and potatoes had been planted and Ambrose was busy earthing-up the potato plants to protect them from late frosts. Beatrice was digging a deep trench; this would be the home of one of her entries for this year's competition: carrots. She had two foes: her carrots needed to

Chapter 1 – Winter to Spring

grow long and she needed to fend off the dreaded carrot fly, a perennial pest to the root crop that left its flesh holed and discoloured. The deep trough, she would fill with soil mixed with coarse grit. She knew that it hadn't to be too rich or the carrots would fork, a catastrophe if she was to win the coveted prize. Carrot flies were a different matter. She'd researched options and decided that she'd sow the carrots lightly, reducing the need to thin them, and she'd erect a fine mesh barrier around the carrots as the pests flew only close to the ground. Later, happy with their progress, Ambrose retired to their bluish grey coloured shed and boiled a kettle on a bottled gas stove. Two mugs of steaming tea were prepared and Ambrose called over to Beatrice who had completed her sturdy fence, a metre high around the freshly sown carrot plot. Beatrice, hair covered with a beret, wearing a blue raincoat and complementing Wellingtons, sauntered over to Ambrose and took the mug from his outstretched hand. "I could do with that, darling."

"You happy?"

"I think that should hold the pests at bay. The potatoes are looking good and broad beans are up. So far, so good," said Beatrice.

"The parsnips are showing too, always slow at germination," said Ambrose, "They need a bit of weeding but I'll leave it until I can see the seedlings a bit better. Leek seeds are sprouting under glass. Just the onions and cabbages and we'll have everything planted for the show." Beatrice was sipping

Chapter 1 – Winter to Spring

her tea, gazing over their allotment, when she mentioned the antics of their competition at number six.

"They've done what?" said Ambrose.

"Reorganised their compost heap. What's that about?" said Beatrice, but the question was rhetorical and she continued, "I need to find out. It might be significant."

~

Towards the end of March, Dolly announced to Betsy that she was visiting her daughter and son in April and would be away for six weeks. Both lived in Australia, having emigrated. Her son, Andrew, lived near Perth and daughter, Diane, was in Sydney. Betsy had commented that it would be nice to stay somewhere between them so that she could pop-in on them both. "It's nearly two and a half thousand miles," said Dolly, "and a four hour plane ride. Anyhow, I can just about afford the journey to Perth. Paying to stay somewhere, well it's out of the question, dear."

Betsy was shocked when she discovered the size of Australia; it was beyond her comprehension, having visited Ostende once and found the food not to her liking. Betsy was at home in Yorkshire, seeing no need to leave its confines, but Dolly's news unsettled her. "Are you only seeing Andrew?" said Betsy, adding, "Diane will be disappointed."

Dolly explained that the trip from the UK to Perth was shorter for her, being almost twenty one hours plus a short stop-off. Betsy's mouth had dropped open when Dolly told her.

Chapter 1 – Winter to Spring

"Nearly a full day on an aeroplane? Are you going to be alright, Dolly?"

Dolly chuckled but she had her own doubts. She and her late husband, Albert hadn't travelled. The farthest they'd gone, when they were much younger, was on a coach ride through France, across the Pyrenees, to Barcelona. They hadn't liked it, found the ferry crossing rough, journey tedious, that the people didn't speak English, and the food strange. They never repeated the experience; Albert liked his home comforts too much. "It'll be fine, dear. Anyhow, Diane is going to come to see me for three weeks while I'm staying with Andrew and his partner. They have an annex, they normally rent it out to folks for their holidays, so I'll have my own space, and I can prepare meals. You know that they're intending to marry this year."

Betsy nodded, unsure what to say, before asking, "What about the grandchildren?"

"They're visiting too, with Diane. It'll be lovely to see them. Their dad, Danny, will take them back after the holiday weekend so they don't miss too much school, but Diane's staying on." Betsy wondered how she'd cope with her best friend away for so long. She wasn't going to rain on Dolly's parade, so she asked her about her preparations and what was planned for her when she arrived down-under. Despite herself, she envied Dolly, and a plan was formulating in her head.

~

A chime sounded as Dolly and Betsy entered the coffee shop and took their customary seats by the window. Betsy peered over toward the far end of the café, spotted the Polish workmen

Chapter 1 – Winter to Spring

and waved at them. Alex strode over to their table. "What brings you back here?" said Betsy.

"A snagging list," said Edwina as she sauntered over to take the order, adding, "Your usual?"

"I was hoping to see you. Not this time, maybe just the tea," said Alex, interrupting the flow.

"I beg your pardon!" said Betsy. In Alex's left hand was a brown paper bag and he opened it, placing the contents on the side plate in front of Betsy.

"There, we do have a bakewell tart," he said, with aplomb.

"That's a cherry bakewell, a common misconception," said Edwina.

"You know that they're not from Bakewell, don't you?" said Betsy, a look of mischief in her eyes, "Another misconception."

"Tea is it?" said Edwina.

Both Betsy and Dolly nodded. Betsy thanked Alex who grinned like a Cheshire cat, and then left the ladies alone. Betsy glanced over at Dolly, who was fiddling with something in her handbag. Hesitant for a moment she gave a small cough and Dolly looked up.

"You look a bit sheepish, Betsy."

"I've something to ask you."

"You don't normally wait, dear. It must be serious."

"I'd like to come to Australia with you," Betsy blurted.

Chapter 1 – Winter to Spring

A look of shock spread across Dolly's face as she mouthed, "But you don't even like leaving Yorkshire."

"I know, but I may not get another chance. If you don't think ..."

Dolly cut into the conversation, saying, "I think it's a wonderful idea, Betsy. Are you sure, it's a long way?"

"What about Andrew?"

"What about Andrew?" repeated Dolly, with a different inflection in her voice.

"Will he mind?"

"I think he'll be delighted, not having to look after his old mum for six weeks. There's plenty of room in their annex for you." The old friends discussed the trip to death and, for the first time in an eternity, Betsy was excited at the prospect of her adventure. Dolly was delighted that she didn't have to endure the trip alone. Any reservations she may have had about Betsy's revelation evaporated as they talked.

Chapter 2 – Spring to Summer

April

  The three allotment holders at number six were busy keeping the weeds at bay, hoeing between the rows of seedlings that would have been at home in a military line up. The April sun was warming the soil and the magical season had begun as each plant raced to grow, ahead of its competitors. The potatoes, earthed up in rows, were showing their tips above the soil, onion stems reaching for the sky, short fuzzy leaves of carrots catching the breeze, red stems of beetroot adding colour, and bright green parsnip leaves advertising their vitality. Bert had mimicked the carrot fly barrier of their rivals, erecting low fencing using fine mesh and a strong wooden frame to survive the westerly winds that gusted between the hills, down the valley. Walter walked over from their shed carrying a tray full of what appeared to be spindly salad onions. They were leek seedlings and he wanted advice from Harold on whether they were ready for planting. Harold examined them and told Walter that they were fine. Walter marked out the row, using two sticks, the remnants of the previous years trimmings, plus a length of green twine. Using a dibber, he made holes at six inch intervals and plonked a leek seedling in each, without adding any soil, leaving a green stem visible. Once he'd planted the row, he watered them and then started on a second. By the time he was finished, it was time for a brew-up and a spot of lunch; Bert and Harold were in the shed already and,

Chapter 2 – Spring to Summer

when Walter entered, a cup of tea was waiting for him. "Thought you'd never finish," said Harold, smiling.

"That looks good," said Walter, picking up the mug and slurping loudly as he drank, "You look tired Bert, are you okay?"

"Oh, just the usual Walter, old age catching up on me. What have you got today?" said Bert, eyeing the box containing Walter's lunch.

"Plantain chips and blackened fish tacos," said Walter, grinning, "I brought some patties for you too, I know you like them."

"Don't mind if I do, I like your spices," said Harold, "Dora's made cake for us. Chocolate." They tucked into their snack, sharing as they always did, while the kettle muttered, heating the water for a second cup of tea, the oil that lubricated Yorkshire society; Black Sheep or Theakston's ale did the same job.

"I think we may have been sold a pup," said Walter.

"What do you mean?" said Bert, yawning.

"The worms. Number thirty haven't touched their compost heap, not since they added the worms."

"It might be a bit early to judge," said Harold, "Anyhow, they haven't done what you've done to ours."

Walter looked over at Harold and then at Bert and nodded, saying, "Aye, you might be right, lads. We've had no run-off from the heap but those worms are doing their work. The

Chapter 2 – Spring to Summer

compost is breaking down. Have you seen how many worms there are now, thousands, must be."

"Their heap's doing the same," said Bert, grinning, "they're multiplying at number thirty, as well."

"You had a look?" said Walter but he needed no reply as Bert's expression answered for him.

"I reckon, they're going for more than the one prize this year," said Bert.

"Dora will have a fit if Beatrice flounces off with another award," said Harold.

"We'd better make sure that that they don't," said Walter as he lit his pipe.

~

"This is good of you, dear," said Dolly.

"My pleasure, have to see you off safely," said Edwina.

They were travelling along the busy M62 motorway across the Pennines. It was Britain's highest motorway, peaking at 1,221 feet, at the aptly named Windy Hill, close to Saddleworth Moor, a bleak barren landscape, notorious for being the location of the burial site of the victims of the sadistic moors murderers, never revealed. Betsy and Dolly were en-route to Manchester airport for their trip to Perth in Australia by Cathay Pacific, stopping briefly to change planes at Hong Kong. Dolly had fussed relentlessly, checking the strange electronic boarding passes that Daniel, the trainee electrician, had helped her print. She'd asked him how they knew they'd board when they hadn't set-off for the airport and he'd laughed in response.

Chapter 2 – Spring to Summer

She was taking her tablet device with her; she used it to contact her son and daughter in Australia, so felt reasonably competent. Daniel gave her a crash course on connecting to public WiFi networks and how to use the free BT service whilst she was abroad. Her head had what she referred to as a muzzy feeling afterwards, and she hoped to remember what he'd told her. Daniel had been patient, later printing out step-by-step instructions, presenting them to Dolly.

Surprisingly, as Betsy was most comfortable in her native Yorkshire, she'd remained unruffled by their trip. Betsy had organised new passports and electronic visas, Daniel rescuing her from the internet soup. She'd packed economically, ensuring that her case was under the measly weight allowance permitted by the airline; she knew that she'd be able to launder her clothes and she didn't own many in any case. She'd paid a trip to the charity shop and bought a couple of frocks plus a jumper; Perth would be entering Autumn and temperatures would fall whilst they were there. Mostly, Betsy was excited by the expedition and early trepidations had vaporised. This was to be her first aeroplane trip, one that would take nearly a day, without cigarettes. Edwina pulled off the motorway into the slip-way that led straight into the airport. She followed the signs to terminal two, past the drop-off point and to the short term parking bays.

"Are you coming in with us?" said Dolly.

"Jane's got the café covered," said Edwina, "I'll help you through check-in and into the departure queue. That's as far as I can go."

Chapter 2 – Spring to Summer

"Let me give you something for the petrol, and parking, at least," said Dolly, Betsy keeping mum.

"You keep your money," said Edwina, feigning indignation, "Spend it when you are in Australia."

They walked from the car to the cavernous check-in lounge, packed with people promenading, like clockwork robots. The information screens showed that their flight check-in counters were numbered from twenty seven to thirty four. Edwina led the way, carrying Dolly and Betsy's regulation size hand luggage, checking that her wards were close behind. Check-in was handled efficiently and Edwina deposited her charges at the entrance to the departure lounge and the security clearance area. Edwina waved until the ladies were out of sight as the line snaked around the corner. She'd done the best that she could but they were now on their own.

~

"They've created a run-off for the compost heap," said Beatrice, leaning on her hoe as Ambrose handed her a cup of steaming coffee, "That tray is supposed to catch the residue."

"It's full of water," said Ambrose.

"Well, it would be, after the torrent last night," said Beatrice.

"I wonder what they're playing at?"

"Search me, but I don't think it's relevant, " said Beatrice.

She sipped the beige coloured liquid from the china mug, pushing her dyed strawberry blond hair back into the brightly coloured wrap that adorned her head. She took a chocolate

Chapter 2 – Spring to Summer

digestive biscuit proffered from a packet in Ambrose's outstretched hand. "They've worms, too," said Ambrose.

"I suppose imitation is the sincerest form of flattery but that'll not help them this year," said Beatrice, dismissively, changing the subject, "Is everything in, except the May sowing, of course?"

Ambrose looked around at the their orderly lines: broad beans, beetroot, carrots, protected by their mesh fence, onions, shallots, leeks, salad crops, cauliflower, savoy cabbage, sprouting broccoli that would be ready for the next season and calabrese. Some of the rows bore exhibition grade seeds; it was these that held their focus, for everything depended upon them for July's competition.

"Just runner beans, courgettes and pumpkins, early May. No pressure for the pumpkins, they won't be ready until autumn."

"Fruit from the garden should finish it, and I'll prepare jam. I have a secret recipe," said Beatrice, smiling.

"You really want to clean-up, this year."

"All of the produce prizes would be nice, but I'm not baking. Let's leave something for the locals."

"Have you heard?" said Ambrose, "I meant to mention it earlier."

What's that?"

"That nice lady, Dolly, she should be on her way to Australia by now. They left today."

Chapter 2 – Spring to Summer

"They?" said Beatrice, suspicious that she knew the answer, "Who's travelling with her?"

"Betsy, her friend, she's going too."

"Odd couple," said Beatrice, "I would never have put them together."

"No," said Ambrose, pondering, "Especially as I don't think Betsy has ever been out of Yorkshire, well not for a long time anyway."

"Should make for an interesting trip," said Beatrice, handing the empty cup back to Ambrose, "but this gossiping won't get the weeding done."

~

The trip through security had been a breeze, except that Betsy was reluctant to place her passport and boarding cards on the tray that the officious officer had supplied. She'd told Dolly that she didn't want them out of her sight and she watched their progress through the x-ray machine before stepping through the scanner herself. Processed as non-hazardous by the airport security apparatchik, she scurried over to the conveyor to collect her possessions, pushing past other travellers. Dolly came through a minute later as Betsy scoured the masses for her friend.

"How could anyone steal anything, and get away, with all of these policemen around?"

"They're not police, and things go missing at airports," said Betsy, gripping tightly to Dolly's arm as they walked into the relative calm of a Mecca of consumerism.

Chapter 2 – Spring to Summer

"You should stop reading those newspapers of yours, they're making you paranoid," said Dolly. Betsy's biggest problem was her noxious habit. Once through security, there would be no opportunity to smoke until she was in Australia, nearly a day later. Daniel had investigated the alternatives for her: electronic cigarettes were not allowed on the plane, nor in the airport, the online consensus was that nicotine patches were useless and most smokers used a diversion tactic of sucking mints or boiled sweets, trying to forget about their craving for the duration. Betsy had decided on the latter approach; more, she saw an opportunity for her to give up her lifetime habit and save herself money, a pragmatic Yorkshire solution.

'Wait in the lounge' was displayed on the display board so the ladies found a seat where they could see the departure instructions. Dolly was in her element as watching people was a favourite pastime. She marvelled at the diversity milling around her; representatives of many of the peoples of the world were present. Her pleasing disposition and welcoming face meant that travellers would talk to her as they transitioned through stages of their journey. Betsy, face naturally stern, thumbed through her Daily Rag, tutting as she consumed another piece of news that reinforced her prejudices. A tubby Irish lady, in her late fifties, weary of her odyssey already, plonked herself heavily onto the seat beside Dolly, placing her hand luggage on the floor and a package that she'd purchased on the shelf between the benches.

"Where are you off to?" she said, turning her head towards Dolly and smiling. She had a lined ruddy complexion, wore

Chapter 2 – Spring to Summer

little make-up, except for a subtle coloured lipstick, and sported a shock of rusty-red hair. Her dress was loose fitting and her shoes flat and sensible for the trip. Dolly told the newcomer that they were travelling to her son's in Perth. Betsy looked up briefly from her newspaper, acknowledged the interloper with a brief nod, before returning to its pages.

"Isn't that the thing, so am I," said the stranger, "but it's a holiday for me. I'm Meara, by the way. I have some friends who moved to Australia. It's time I went to see them."

Dolly introduced herself, plus the reluctant Betsy, and they talked the type of conversation that was the lubrication of civilisation: many words, little information and soon forgotten. Meara was flying with a different airline to Dolly and Betsy and her gate was displayed earlier. Unsteadily, she pulled herself to her feet and picked up her bag, placing it clumsily on her shoulder. "It was lovely to talk to you, hope to see you in Australia," were her last words as she shuffled away.

Twenty minutes later the board displayed the departure gate for Dolly and Betsy's flight. They gathered up their possessions, stood and Betsy did her customary glance around, to check that they hadn't left anything behind. It was then that she spotted Meara's package and, not wanting any tensions, decided to say nothing to Dolly. Betsy linked arms with her, glancing upwards for directions to their gate.

~

The gate was a distance away and, by the time they reached it, the ladies were exhausted and flustered as they had heard their name mentioned over the public address system: 'Would

Chapter 2 – Spring to Summer

Mrs Jackson and Mrs Longbottom make their way immediately to gate 208 where your flight is waiting to depart.' The charming steward from Cathay Pacific smiled as the women approached and held out her hand for their travel papers. She kept their boarding cards and replaced them with new ones, scanned them and indicated that Betsy and Dolly were to follow her. Half way down the ramp a photographer stopped them and took a picture of the ladies with the ground steward. "Would you mind if I asked a couple of questions?" the photographer said.

He was wearing a Cathay Pacific uniform, of Chinese origin and smiling profusely. "What kind of questions? We're in a hurry young man," said Betsy.

The photographer glanced at the steward who nodded and said, "Be brief please, they are waiting."

The photographer asked Dolly about her trip and her family but spent most of his time talking to Betsy. He seemed fascinated that she should be undertaking such a long haul journey at her time of life and her first flight. Betsy faked indignation but was secretly delighted by the interest that the man was displaying. An air steward popped his head around the corner of the 'plane ramp and the lady from the ground staff understood the gesture. She ushered Dolly and Betsy down the tunnel into the awaiting Boeing 777 and handed her charges over to the flight attendant who inspected their boarding cards again. To the ladies surprise, they turned left after they entered the aeroplane and into a spacious cabin reserved for business class travellers.

Chapter 2 – Spring to Summer

"It's bigger than I thought," said Betsy, "and plenty of leg room."

"I think we're in the wrong place," said Dolly, turning to the air steward striding ahead of them, stopping at two seats near the front of the fuselage.

"I don't think this is right, dear," said Dolly to the attendant.

The hostess looked at the boarding cards again, saying, "Definitely, these are your seats. I have a message from the ground staff for you, a question really. The photos they took were for the in-flight magazine. The photographer forgot to ask your permission to use them, plus the interview. If you are happy, I'll bring an agreement form for you during the flight. Let me know later but, for now, as we're near departure, can I get you a drink? There's champagne, bucks fizz, juice or water.

"How much will that be?" said Betsy.

"It's complementary madam," said the attendant, smiling, "Now, can I take your jacket?"

~

Walter was leaning against his hoe, standing on the grass path that separated the allotments. Harold was between the rows of broad beans, now a few inches high, hoe resting in the well of his arm. The weather was bright but a gusty wind blew from the east, making it feel cooler by a couple of degrees. They'd been discussing Dolly and Betsy, gallivanting off to Australia. Dora had called them mad-as-hatters for undertaking the journey 'at their age, should know better'. Harold thought differently: he admired their courage, tinged with envy. He

Chapter 2 – Spring to Summer

knew that he'd not be able to coax Dora any further than Scarborough or Bridlington, and then only once in the year. Walter was sanguine. If the women wanted to go to Australia, then good for them, but it wasn't something he was considering any time soon. He was more concerned about the state of his compost heap; he knew the worms were a disaster, but he hadn't admitted it to anyone else. That day, Bert was at his brother's house with his wife, Elsie, the plot being manned by Walter and Harold. Their focus was weeding. Weeds sapped the energy of their crops and were enemy number one, followed closely by the pigeons. These, and other avian creatures, were deterred by old CDs and tinfoil trays that swayed in the wind, suspended from clothes line like structures strung across the allotment. Their atomic weapon hung from a tall mast and was a kite in the shape of a bird of prey. The breeze caused it to swoop and dive; it was the most effective of their armaments.

"Carrots are a bit thin, yet," said Walter, not wishing to discuss the compost pile.

"It's early. A bit of heat will see them right," said Harold, "Onions looking good, sprouting nicely."

"Number thirty is the same, their carrots look a bit insipid," said Walter.

Harold peered at Walter, who knew what was coming. "We can't put it off for ever, Walter."

"The blasted worms, you mean?"

Harold nodded as Walter replied, "I'll accept the evidence, it's not working. I can't see how they'll give us an advantage this year." He went on to explain that he'd been watching their

Chapter 2 – Spring to Summer

competition and they'd done nothing with their worm infested organic fertiliser heap, except to remove the tarpaulin. Walter suggested they do the same. Harold wasn't keen and wanted to finish his hoeing, but he humoured Walter. They ambled over to the heap and peeled back the cover. Steam surged out as they removed more of the sheet. Walter commented that the compost was doing its job; warmth meant decomposition, which meant good compost, free of weed seeds. Heat presaged a different fate for the worms. A rummage confirmed their fears; the worms had scarpered or perished. A gust of wind caught the tarpaulin which lifted into the air, floated over their neighbours allotment, then the next, landing on number thirty, demolishing the carrot-fly fence and squashing the seedlings. Taking to the air again, it cleared the canal and disappeared into the fields beyond. Walter and Harold stared at each other, dumbstruck for a moment. Then Walter glanced around at the empty allotment. Except for Harold and himself, nobody had seen the incident. Harold nodded, perceptive to his friend's thoughts. "Best keep mum, eh?"

"Yes, but let's fetch the tarpaulin. Don't want any evidence."

~

The flight had been just over eleven and a half hours to Hong Kong where the Dolly and Betsy would change planes. Their schedule had given them an hour for the transfer but there had been a delay. They now had just over four hours in the transit area of Hong Kong's airport. The purser had been attentive to the ladies during the flight, explaining that Dolly's son had pulled some strings, upgrading their journey to Business Class

Chapter 2 – Spring to Summer

for the flight from Manchester, and the one out of Hong Kong. As they'd started their descent into 'the other China', as Betsy called it, the attendant had told them of their onward delay. She also informed them that they could use the executive lounge, where they could freshen up, or have a shower. Betsy's face twisted at the thought as Dolly thanked the steward.

"I'll have to see if I can contact Andrew, tell him about the delay," said Dolly as she was interrupted by an announcement from the flight crew leader telling them to refasten their seatbelts. The plane tipped downward and a change in engine noise told of their descent. A nail biting eternity later, in reality thirty minutes, the Boeing 777 wheels touched the ground lightly, brakes were applied and a roar of reverse thrust from the engines sounded. Betsy breathed a sigh of relief as her heart rate started to return to normal. She glanced at Dolly, surprised at her friend's pale complexion, but hers was no different.

~

"I've been following the flight, mum," said the image of Andrew as Dolly and Betsy sat in the business class lounge, utilising the free WiFi with Dolly's tablet, "I know you're delayed. Don't worry, we'll be there to meet you. How's the trip been."

"Oh, Andrew it has been wonderful. There were films, meals were nice, free drinks and, would you credit it, the seats slid down to make a bed. I could stretch out and that nice steward brought me a blanket. It was a bit noisy, but I did manage to sleep. Wasn't keen on the landing. Did you get us into business class, Andrew?"

Chapter 2 – Spring to Summer

"Glad you liked it," said Andrew, "John suggested the upgrade. Couldn't have you coming all of this way in coach."

"I don't think they run a coach, dear. How long would it take, I wonder?"

Andrew laughed as his mother thanked him for their added luxury. His last words, before Dolly disconnected the call were, "Just enjoy the flight. Don't worry, we'll monitor it and we'll definitely be there to pick up you and Betsy. Love you mum, safe journey."

Dolly decided to avail herself of the washing facilities. Betsy declined, telling Dolly that she would protect their belongings. Dolly was certain that nobody would attempt to interfere with any of their luggage, especially with Betsy guarding it. Freshening her tea cup before Dolly left, Betsy settled back with a Woman's Magazine that she'd collected from the display near the entrance. A man walked along the isle with a glass of water and took a seat to her left in the crowded lounge.

"Are you travelling alone?" he said, in a cultured English accent.

"What's it to you," said Betsy, glancing briefly at him.

"I'm sorry, I didn't mean to interrupt. Where are you travelling to?"

"Australia, Perth."

"I see that you are not an aficionado of small talk. Is that a Yorkshire accent, I detect, North Yorkshire if I am not mistaken."

"West Riding, now North Yorkshire, yes."

Chapter 2 – Spring to Summer

"Did you travel from Leeds airport. My, how it has grown."

"Manchester."

"Were you caught in that rumpus, did it delay you?"

"What rumpus?" said Betsy, turning her head towards the man for the first time, placing the magazine on her lap.

"There was a bomb scare, I read. A suspicious parcel. Turned out to be a gift that someone left behind. I'm Eugene by the way."

"Delighted, I'm sure," said Betsy, as she introduced herself, desperately hoping that Dolly would return soon.

The man was grey haired, smartly dressed in a pin-striped suit, pink shirt with a white collar, blue silk tie and his charcoal coloured overcoat was strewn across the adjacent chair. "I'm heading in the opposite direction. Just returned from Sydney, business there, home to London now. Are you visiting family?"

"My friend, Dolly. She has a son and daughter in Australia. I'm accompanying her."

"How long are you staying?"

"Six weeks."

"A gruelling flight, straight through is it?"

"Yes, we're delayed."

Betsy returned to her magazine and Eugene understood the nuanced message, picking up his copy of the Economist as he sipped his water. As Dolly returned, the gentleman stood and wished the ladies a *bon voyage*. Dolly glanced at Betsy as she said, when he was out of earshot, "Who was that?"

Chapter 2 – Spring to Summer

"Started talking to me. Full of his own importance," said Betsy, "How was the shower?"

"Wonderful," said Dolly, "The towels were crisp white and luxurious. Soap, shampoo, conditioner, cologne and hand crème, all available for free."

"Doesn't look like you've washed your hair," said Betsy.

"I've just had it set," said Dolly, smiling, "I used their hairnet. I've kept it, might come in handy."

Betsy grinned and restarted reading her magazine. She'd keep the news about the bomb scare at Manchester airport to herself.

~

"Who would do such a thing?" It was eight o'clock in the morning and Beatrice was standing by the row of carrots, on the path at the edge of their allotment, examining the devastation. The pest barrier was down and one of the upright supporting posts had snapped. Worse, most of the seedlings had been flattened and would need to be resown. The question in Beatrice's mind was 'is there enough time?' Defeat was not an option for her: pride was at stake, there had to be a way. Ambrose peered at his wife of countless years as her demeanour set and then altered. A look of unease sailed across his face and intensified as Beatrice smiled. She strode from their plot, instructing Ambrose to follow. Later, they returned with a new purchase: a poly-tunnel, six foot high, the same width and a length that almost spanned the allotment's breadth. They spent the afternoon erecting it and would return the following morning to sow their crops within. Beatrice had

Chapter 2 – Spring to Summer

learned her lesson; she would have contingency and an excess of produce. She would win, there was no other way, whatever the cost.

~

"What've they done now?" said Bert, "Is that allowed?"

"No regulations against it," said Harold, "Our Dora's checked. She says that old Ben has installed a poly-tunnel on his plot. Got his from a farmer friend, was past its best."

"That one looks brand new," said Walter, "We can't compete with that."

"We can't see what they're doing inside it either. This is bad news, and what happened to their carrots?" said Bert.

Harold glanced sheepishly at Walter and they both shrugged, Harold adding, "They say it could have been a deer."

"Don't seem to have touched anything else," said Bert, "We don't usually have them round here?"

"That's what people are suggesting," said Walter, swiftly changing the subject, "Our plants have been spared, thankfully. Look, that monstrosity on number thirty has given me an idea. We still have those cloches, don't we?" A feature of allotmenteers is that they scrounge anything. The cloches, metal wires covered in thick plastic, with prongs used to secure them in the soil, were surplus when a local nursery closed. They'd seen better days but were part of a tactic of make-do-and-mend adopted by the pensioners. Walter suggested that they be put into service to encourage their insipid carrot seedlings to develop. An exhausted Bert

Chapter 2 – Spring to Summer

grumbled, hoping that Walter's inspiration would perform better than had the worms. By the end of the afternoon, the carrots were watered and covered in their protective layer and Walter's hopes were high that his ploy would work this time.

~

Dolly was excited as they touched town at Perth's International Airport, around seven miles from the compact city of Perth in Western Australia, the country's famous wine growing area. They disembarked and headed for immigration where their papers were processed efficiently by friendly officers, respectful of the pensioners' age and separation from their own time zone. He'd given them a smiling 'G'day ladies' as he pointed in the direction of the baggage collection area. A young man helped Dolly with her case, leaving Betsy to collect her own, though he assisted her to place it on a wheeled cart that Betsy steered towards the exit. They read the dire warnings about the penalties for bringing fresh produce into Australia, for disease prevention, and Dolly asked Betsy several times if she had any fruit or vegetables. Betsy ignored her friend, pushing onward towards the 'nothing to declare' doorway. The final exit slid open to reveal an expansive area populated with throngs of people awaiting the arrival of their relatives or friends. The experience was overwhelming as Dolly scanned the faces for her son, a man in his forties, balding, a neatly trimmed beard, all grey coloured, last seen by Skype from Hong Kong. As Betsy wheeled the trolley along the twisty channel, Andrew stepped forward and hugged his mother, depositing a kiss on her left cheek. He then welcomed Betsy,

Chapter 2 – Spring to Summer

making her uncomfortable with a similar greeting. Andrew asked about the journey, their health and other chitchat as he took control of the luggage cart and led the ladies through the airport. As they reached the payment-point for the car park, Dolly spotted Andrew's partner and she made a beeline for him. They embraced and John stepped back, still holding Dolly by her hands.

"My, you don't look like you've just flown half way around the world." His voice was husky, matching his tall, slim, muscular build. He sported a head of closely trimmed red hair, pale complexion and was clean shaven. He was a few years younger than Andrew and they'd been together for at least fifteen years. Dolly introduced Betsy, who smiled, but her face was not made that way, preferring to frown. John was oblivious to her demeanour and gave the hapless Betsy a hug, planting a sloppy kiss on her cheek.

"Has Andrew told you?" said John, portraying excitement.

"Give me a chance," said Andrew, smiling at his partner, "We've arranged our marriage, while you are here, mum. I want you to be part of it, now that Australia has caught up with the UK. You too Betsy." They were referring to Australia's landmark decision to allow same-sex marriage, following in the footsteps of many liberal countries around the world. Dolly was in raptures at the news, a smile embellishing her face during the journey to Freemantle, where Andrew and John lived, on the southern side of the Swan River and South West of the city of Perth. The smile slid when she fell asleep, snoring gently, as they hit State Route 7.

Chapter 2 – Spring to Summer

~

"The forecast is bad," said Harold.

The three allotment holders were seated around a table, the varnish having seen better days, in 'The Old Oak', a free house, one of a dwindling number of public houses in Heythwaite. Bert put down the pint of his usual best bitter that he'd just supped and said, "Tomorrow, late frost, minus two they said. Just the potatoes we'll need to watch."

"You're out, aren't you?" said Walter, as Harold nodded, "I'll pop over in the afternoon and put some fleece over them. There's too much green now to cover them with dirt."

"I'll come along, give you a hand," said Bert.

Walter smiled as he looked at his watch, which showed seven thirty, saying, "Best go and join the rabble."

"Drink up, then," said Harold, "I'll ask Graham for refills."

It was the Allotment Growers' Association annual general and committee meeting that evening, being held in the upstairs private room. Payment of subscriptions was due; the AGM was also the time when plot holders registered for the summer competition, a ploy to ensure that everyone attended and paid-up. The meeting started at eight o'clock but the three friends needed to be early. That ensured that they took their usual position, in the second row, centre, of the ten rows of seats. When they entered the room, Ambrose and Beatrice were seated already in their prized chairs. Walter glanced at Harold and Bert, who shook their heads. Bert marched to the front and took equivalent seats in the front row, that way they wouldn't

Chapter 2 – Spring to Summer

have to look at the back of their adversaries' heads. Walter acknowledged the couple, the only other people in the room, with 'now then', a familiar Yorkshire greeting, and Harold did the same, but with a mumble. Bert ignored Ambrose and Beatrice, landing heavily on the chair in front of Beatrice, placing his glass on the floor in front of him. It wasn't long before the room started to fill with other allotment holders who greeted each other warmly, or in a perfunctory manner. The three amigos were popular and others came over to speak to them about the contradictions of the weather, crops, growing conditions and general gardening talk. Beatrice and Ambrose seemed isolated, except among the committee grandees, where they were more comfortable. Five minutes before the meeting commenced, the chair, Town Councillor Amanda Braithwaite, banged on the table with her gavel and spoke in her broad West Yorkshire accent.

"Five minutes. If you need a comfort break or another drink, now's the time. We'll start in five minutes, sharp." The councillor, true to her word, commenced proceedings at eight o'clock. After the usual formalities, the subject of payment of subscriptions was the first main item on the agenda. Two payments were due: fees for the allotment to the Town Council and the annual contribution to running the Allotment Growers' Association. This being Yorkshire, much discussion was initiated on the level of the trivial charge made by the association and where the money was spent. The much larger rental charge for the allotment plot, with its five percent increase, passed without a mutter. The chair deferred to the

Chapter 2 – Spring to Summer

treasurer to explain the dull finances of the association while members glanced at his reports, their eyes glazing over.

Until his last comment.

"Finally, ladies and gentlemen, the committee has decided that only plot holders who are fully paid up, no arrears, will be permitted to enter competitions. The regulations have been updated, requiring only a majority of the elected committee's agreement, and will be applied immediately."

A murmur of conversation circled the room and the meeting chair struck her mallet on the table again to bring order. "Before we move on, are there any questions?"

Walter, Harold and Bert had not paid their Town Council allotment dues for the past five years; in the true fashion of the region, they'd used the inefficiency of officialdom to keep money in their own pocket, rather than into the coffers of the already wealthy, as they saw it. They were a hundred and fifty pounds in arrears and they were not alone. A question came from an allotment holder, concerned that he wouldn't be able to register for the championship that evening. He wanted to know how long he had to clear the financial obligation.

"We're aware of the situation," Councillor Braithwaite said, her voice betraying impatience, "We've decided that members can record their wish to enter the summer competition this evening. Those who have no arrears, or have cleared their debts by the end of May, will be confirmed. Now, we must move on. The next item is the election of officers to committee positions."

Chapter 2 – Spring to Summer

The situation was bad, but then it became worse as the three friends watched in disbelief as Beatrice was proposed, seconded and then elected onto the committee of the Allotment Growers' Association.

~

Andrew and John's home was in Freemantle, close to Point Walter on the busy Burke Drive, overlooking the Swan river and Perth beyond. It was single story, set back off the road, with a modest rear garden that John remarked was 'enough' as they were both busy working, not having the time to do it justice. The front garden was paved and a place to park Andrew and John's vehicles, the sizeable garage being used mostly as overflow storage. A glass covered open walkway, separated the main house from the annex, another single story construction with two bedrooms, a combined lounge, diner, kitchen and a spacious bathroom with a walk-in shower. Betsy and John struck an accord immediately, especially when John told Betsy about his delight that she'd visited with her friend, pleased that Dolly would have company when they were working. He'd said that he and Andrew would take some vacation time but that it would be limited, especially as they were having a honeymoon after the wedding, in Fiji. The ceremony would be held towards the end of their trip and Diane, Dolly's daughter, had changed her plans, deciding to visit two weeks prior, with Danny and the grandchildren travelling for the wedding. To the tired ladies these events seemed an age away; all they wanted was to put their heads down on a pillow and catch up on their beauty sleep.

Chapter 2 – Spring to Summer

~

Andrew was home the day after Dolly and Betsy's arrival and he fussed over them, making breakfast and taking them into Freemantle's famous Cappuccino Strip for a stroll and lunch. Though it was autumn in the Southern Hemisphere, the weather was kind: sunny, a perfect temperature, light breeze and dry. More like a Yorkshire summer than the fall season.

"John and I have to work for the rest of the week, mum," said Andrew as they completed their meal.

"Don't you worry, dear. We'll find plenty to occupy ourselves. It's just nice to be here with you."

"Are there buses?" said Betsy.

Public transport ran frequently within the city but not where Andrew lived. Dolly hadn't driven for years and wasn't keen on driving in Australia. Andrew knew this, so had arranged for Janet, their long-time cleaner, to act as a taxi service for his guests. He'd given Dolly a pay-as-you-go mobile phone with important numbers programmed into it: Andrew's cell phone, John's mobile, Janet's phone number, a local taxi firm and one for the emergency services. "You've thought of everything," said Betsy, smiling as she pulled herself into the rear of the car, to return to the house.

The following day, Janet arrived after breakfast, popping her head round the door as Dolly was washing the dishes. She was attractive, in her fifties, died blond hair held up by clips, gaunt, with skin finely lined by exposure to the sun and much smiling. She wore a blue floral patterned apron over a blouse and loose

Chapter 2 – Spring to Summer

fitting trousers, finished with flat heeled brown shoes. "Oh, you should have left them for me. I'm Janet, hope Andrew mentioned me. You must be his mum, I can see the resemblance."

"He's more like his Dad," said Dolly, drying her hands so that she could greet the newcomer properly.

"Such a nice couple, and you're here for the wedding, too. That'll be nice for them both."

Betsy emerged from the bedroom and Dolly introduced Janet to her. "Pleased, I'm sure," said Betsy.

Janet, not quite sure how to react, did what any self-respecting Australian would have done, beamed and said, "G'day, you enjoying yourself?"

After a period of chitchat, they negotiated a trip into Freemantle where they'd hop on a bus into the City of Perth to see the sights. Dolly was keen to visit the Botanic Gardens at Kings Park. Janet was unsure whether she should leave the women to their own devices but Betsy was quite insistent, as was Dolly, and changing their minds was not an option. On the way, Janet explained the bus system, the routes, ticket buying, where to alight for Kings Park and where to pick up the bus for the return trip. With trepidation, she waved at the ladies as she left them at the bus stop.

~

Kings Park was a delight, perched high on the Mount Eliza escarpment and free-of-charge, much to the satisfaction of Betsy. It was huge, covering over a thousand acres, larger than

Chapter 2 – Spring to Summer

New York's central park as the girl in the visitors' centre was chuffed to tell the ladies. It overlooked Perth and the Swan River, wide at this point. Dolly's favourite part was the Western Australia Botanic Gardens, containing a collection of indigenous plants, many endangered and housed in the Conservation Gardens. The upside-down looking Giant Boab tree, broad trunk and branches that resembled roots, designed for dry conditions, caught Betsy's eye. She'd seen one on television; somehow, seeing it 'for real' was special. The weather was perfect: clear blue sky, wonderful visibility, a fine temperature for walking, and dry. As they strolled towards the Botanical Cafe, to rest their feet and quench their thirst, they walked past a film crew, interviewing an Australian personality not known to Dolly or Betsy. The camera had the logo of the Australian Broadcasting Corporation on its side; the brand was also worn by the squad, on the back of their shirts, but not by the interviewer, a woman, smartly dressed in blue business-style clothes and black high-heel shoes. She was a brunette, sported blue rimmed spectacles, and bright red lipstick. A few young, mixed-sex, protesters held up placards, objecting to the cost of University fees. Betsy asked one of the female demonstrators why they were complaining. As she was explaining, a man, in his late twenties, started shouting at the students. He'd been drinking and was mouthing profanities, telling the protesters that they were work-shy layabouts. He lunged forward, aiming for the girl who was talking to Betsy. Dolly spotted him and lifted her hand bag, striking him squarely on the top of his lowered head. He turned towards her, as she delivered a second swipe, across his face. Two of the

Chapter 2 – Spring to Summer

students, both male, dropped their banners and stepped forward to restrain the assailant. The security guards soon appeared and whisked him away. The television cameras were no longer on the politician being interviewed; they had followed the rumpus and Dolly had been caught on-camera, defending the student's honour. "Are you alright?" said the girl as the interviewer reached Dolly and Betsy.

"Don't fuss, dear," said Dolly, holding on to Betsy's arm, "I'm perfectly fine." Betsy led Dolly over to a bench and, once seated, Dolly caught her breath. The TV interviewer sat next to Dolly, Betsy on the other side, her entourage of camera and sound men joined them, and the cameras rolled. The questions followed: what they'd seen, what happened, where they were from, how long they'd been in Perth and what they thought of the City? When it was all over and the flighty media moved on to their next story, Dolly looked at Betsy, smiling as she spoke. "I think I could manage that cup of tea now."

~

There had been a light drizzle earlier but it had cleared and sunshine shone sporadically through the broken cloud. The plants in the ground of Walter, Bert and Harold's allotment, seedlings no more for they were growing well, soaked up the life giving elixir; the miracle of photosynthesis, where plant growth came from the air, in the form of carbon dioxide, water, sunshine and a few important nutrients from the soil, supplying animals with oxygen in return. The three men were seated on a wooden bench, retrieved from a skip and re-purposed, peering out over their rapidly growing produce. Weeds seemed to

Chapter 2 – Spring to Summer

outperform the crops and needed to be continually kept in check. Each of the pensioners had watched in bewilderment the previous evening's news bulletins. On their screens, as large as life, from the other side of the globe, were two Yorkshire women, talking on Australian television, appearing on the main bulletins and invited to the set of a breakfast show too. The announcer had said that the same women had featured in the Cathay Pacific in-flight magazine. They didn't know what to make of it all.

"Did you see Dolly attacking that drunk with her bag?" said Walter, "If it had been that Betsy lass, I wouldn't have been surprised, but Dolly, well!"

"They caused a bit of a stir, by all accounts," said Bert, "Criticising the Australian education system."

"To be fair to Betsy, what she said was that we should be investing in our kids, not loading them with debt," said Harold, "She told them it was the same in Britain, and that it wasn't right."

"It was when she told them that students were being taught the wrong things. Betsy told them that science, engineering, health, farming and other trades, were what was needed. When she asked how many more overpaid footballers or TV presenters were required, I thought that telly host was going to explode," said Walter.

"Good for her, is all I say," said Bert, "My Elsie says the same. Betsy's only saying what people think."

Chapter 2 – Spring to Summer

"It'll soon blow over," said Harold, "You know what they're like, attention span of a gnat, or shorter."

"I hope you're talking about the media and not our Dolly and Betsy," said Bert, laughing.

"Wouldn't dare say anything to Betsy's face," said Harold, grinning.

~

"It's in the papers too," said Beatrice, pointing to an article in the Observer newspaper that she was reading. She and Ambrose were in their library, a room embellished with wall-to-wall bookcases, stacked with tomes of every kind and carefully catalogued, labels indicating the type of books contained on the shelves. One told of history volumes, another of gardening and the fiction shelves were arranged in author order. At the centre of the room were two comfortable over-stuffed armchairs, a small table beside each one. Ambrose and Beatrice had seen the television coverage of Dolly and Betsy's episode in Kings Park in Perth and Beatrice was reading an article about it.

"The article talks of a group of drunks," said Beatrice, "That's not what appeared on the TV."

"You know the papers, it's all about sensationalism and selling newspapers," said Ambrose, "She gave that chap a right belt with that handbag. Good for her."

Beatrice smiled and glanced at her husband, "Had that been the other woman, I wouldn't have been surprised, but that delightful old lady, well, I wouldn't have expected it from her."

Chapter 2 – Spring to Summer

"Probably spur of the moment, instinct kicked in. They're celebrities down-under now."

"I'm sure we'll hear all about it when they return," said Beatrice, turning over the page to read another feature.

~

Andrew and John's emotions about the Kings Park event were difficult to classify: concern for the women's welfare, guilt at abandoning them, anger at the danger they encountered and pride at their courage. Diane's was easier to comprehend: annoyed that Andrew had allowed the ladies to be put in danger. She berated her brother, deciding to travel earlier so that she could 'look after her mother', the implication being that Andrew could not. Dolly was distraught that her actions was causing sibling tensions and she did her best to calm troubled waters in a call to Diane. She decided to shun any further media interviews, though the brouhaha they'd caused was receding, the news outlets moving on, as they did. Betsy stepped in to the impasse and recruited John as an ally. Diane was unable to travel until the following week, leaving a window of opportunity, as tempers calmed. Betsy suggested that the cleaner, Janet, act as a chaperone for her and Dolly until Diane arrived. "It doesn't have to be real," said Betsy, grinning as she spoke, "Only as far as Diane is concerned."

"I see, and Janet needs to be complicit, is that what you are saying?" said John.

"You are following me, then," said Betsy, "What do you think?"

Chapter 2 – Spring to Summer

"It could work," said John, musing, scratching his end of day red stubble, "If Andrew agrees."

"We have to tell him?" said Betsy, a glint in her eye.

The ruse worked, harmony returning to the Jackson family, Diane keeping her original travel arrangements, and John telling Andrew about the subterfuge, not willing to hoodwink his partner. Andrew kept the knowledge to himself and Dolly was oblivious to the deception, happy that balance had returned. Their celebrity status did not wane, especially in Freemantle. In restaurants, stores and coffee shops, Dolly and Betsy were stopped and asked about their experience; 'Good on'ya' was the oft repeated soliloquy. Andrew and John's cleaner, Janet, became a good friend of the ladies during their stay, sometimes joining them on their outings when she had little work. On one occasion, she took them south, around fifty miles away, to the city of Mandurah, a wealthy coastal resort. "How about seeing some dolphins?" said Janet as she pulled into the car park.

"That sounds wonderful, dear," said Dolly.

Janet explained that Mandurah Cruises had regular boats leaving from the city. Elucidating, she said that the trips would last about an hour and were on the inland waterways, so the going wouldn't be rough. "If we take the noon trip, we can eat on board. How does that sound?"

Betsy was having none of it, not happy with eating on the boat, it didn't seem right, she thought. They decided that they'd take the afternoon trip, giving them a chance to look around the stunning harbour first. The marina was packed with expensive

Chapter 2 – Spring to Summer

boats, affluence exuding from its pores, the fantastic weather adding to the magical sight of hundreds of masts glinting in the sun as they gently swayed. A grey haired gentleman sporting a close cropped beard was brushing the surface of the deck of a yacht with a stiff brush. He looked up as the three women strolled by, nodded a greeting and returned to his cleaning. He glanced up again as the ladies reached the stern of his yacht.

"Didn't I see you on TV?"

Betsy turned first and said, "Well, you might have done."

"Ah, the north of England accent, unmistakable. Why don't you join us for a drink. Coffee, tea, or something stronger?"

"A tea would be delightful, if you're sure," said Dolly.

The man called below deck and a tanned and deeply creased woman climbed up the steps from below. Her long hair was tidied with plastic grip-clips and was dyed like a red-head. "You're the two Yorkshire women, clobbered that drunk in Perth. I saw you on the television," she said, glancing at Dolly and Betsy, "Good on'ya. You gave him a sore head."

"This is Babs and I'm Jimmy," said the man, "Sorry you had to experience all of that. Let me get those drinks. Tea you said? What about you?"

Betsy requested tea and Janet, amused by her charge's notoriety, sought coffee. Jimmy helped his guests aboard the yacht, found them seats around a small table at the stern, and then descended into the galley to make the drinks. Babs chatted to the three ladies until Jimmy reappeared with steaming mugs and a tray of 'Tim Tams', arguably Australia's favourite biscuit.

Chapter 2 – Spring to Summer

Jimmy and Babs were in their sixties and had been in Australia since they were children, never having known their native Lancashire. Their parents each brought them down-under, sometime in the late fifties, under the 'ten pound POMS' scheme of the Australian government, intended to encourage British citizens to settle in Australia. They'd done well, making a good living, transporting goods around the world.

"Where are you from?" said Jimmy.

"Yorkshire," said Betsy.

"I know that," said Jimmy, smiling, "Whereabouts in that fine county, second only to Lancashire."

Betsy gave her host a sideways glance and he felt the proverbial ice under his feet thinning, as she replied, "I think not! Heythwaite, you probably haven't heard of it, near Skipton."

"On the contrary," said Jimmy but he was interrupted by his wife.

"We did a cruise in the Mediterranean, last year. There were a group of Yorkshire folks on the trip. I'm sure they were from Heythwaite."

"They were, Babs," said Jimmy.

Dolly glanced at Betsy as she peered at Jimmy, Janet looking on, bemused. "Dick, Madge, George, Alistair and Catherine, is that right?" said Dolly.

"Catherine had cancer. How is she now?" said Babs.

"She died," said Betsy.

Chapter 2 – Spring to Summer

Dolly jumped in quickly, saying, "They took the trip to spend some time together. Alastair didn't have much of that, a farmer, you know, works all hours, in all conditions." Jimmy nodded as Dolly continued, "He's a grandfather, grandson arrived just before we left."

"That's some comfort, I suppose," said Babs.

The mood was becoming sombre so Janet interjected, attempting to lighten the tone by asking the yacht owners whether they'd enjoyed their cruise. Images were described of red sunsets, crystal blue waters, first views of distant lands and the whitewashed Mediterranean houses, clearly visible as they sailed into port. The reminiscences gushed. Then followed descriptions of the wild life they'd witnessed: dolphins, swordfish, white sharks and even a loggerhead turtle. "Magical," said Babs.

"Except for one incident, soon forgotten, no harm done." said Jimmy.

"What was that?" said Betsy.

"Oh, I had a bag filched, in Mallorca. Someone ripped it from my shoulder. More an inconvenience than anything else."

Babs glanced at Jimmy as she said, "Hardly that. We haven't been able to open the safe since."

"We took the keys to the safe we keep at the bank with us, ironically to prevent it being stolen while we were away. It was in the bag and the bank won't replace it."

"What was in the box?" said Betsy, Dolly uncomfortable that Betsy was asking the question but wanting to know the answer.

Chapter 2 – Spring to Summer

"Sentimental stuff, valuable to us, but not to anyone else," said Babs as she changed the subject, asking about the women's plans. They discussed the forthcoming wedding, visit of Dolly's daughter and grandchildren and date of their return to Yorkshire, as they finished their drinks. Then Janet indicated that they needed to rush to make the afternoon boat for the cruise to experience the dolphins. Thanking their hosts for the refreshments, Dolly and Betsy, followed by Janet, stepped onto the gangplank, and then the quay. "Please give my regards on to our cruise companions," were Jimmy's last words as he passed a business card to Dolly.

"That was a bit of a coincidence," Janet said as Dolly opened the car door and Betsy glanced at Dolly and nodded.

~

The ladies discussed their chance meeting with Jimmy and Babs, deciding to ask Dick or Alastair some questions when they returned to Heythwaite. Dolly had studied Jimmy's business card. It was innocuous, light blue, one side showing his image, captaining the yacht they'd boarded, with his name in bold classy lettering, a telephone number, e-mail address, and the by-line 'J.L. Myerscough & Son, Specialists in Domestic and International Freight'. On the other side was a Perth office address and a location on the web. They had little time to think further about their encounter as Andrew took a week away from work and was determined to show his mother and Betsy the sights of Western Australia, wearing them out in the process. Again, they journeyed south, past Mandurah, to Bunbury where they saw wild bottlenose dolphins swimming

Chapter 2 – Spring to Summer

close to Koombana beach. Next, they travelled through the Eucalyptus forests, heading towards Albany, stopping at Walpole for the night, as Andrew had a surprise for them the following day. They stayed at a boutique hotel, checking-in close to dusk. Andrew was relieved that they had arrived before darkness fell. The owner of the guest house told Dolly that the road into Walpole was dangerous during nightfall as kangaroos strayed onto it, attracted by vehicle lights. There had been several accidents caused by collisions between the marsupials and cars, some fatal. Dolly asked the proprietor where they could see kangaroos and she told her that they were everywhere. "If you are willing to get up early, six o'clock, you're certain to find them on the golf course, just outside of Walpole," she said, raising her eyebrows, "Lots of them!"

That's how Betsy, Dolly and Andrew found themselves, parked up at the golfing range early the following morning. The low sun cast long shadows and the light was perfect. The ladies watched in fascination as hundreds of 'roos jumped, hopped and ambled across the course, sometimes stopping to nibble vegetation, oblivious to the presence of the vehicle. Later, at breakfast, an excited Dolly commented to a waiter about their dawn outing and sightings. "Ah, hell," he said, "I have 'roos in my garden every day."

Andrew smiled as Betsy retorted, "Well, young man, we don't!"

Outside of Walpole was a world famous tree-top walk, in the Valley of the Giants, and the reason that Andrew made the trip. He'd arranged for them to visit but became apprehensive when

Chapter 2 – Spring to Summer

he told his mum and Betsy what he had planned. "How high?" asked Dolly.

"Forty metres, that's all," said Andrew, "and it's designed for visitors of all ages. You'll kick yourselves if you don't see it, now we are so close."

Betsy was keener than Dolly on the adventure; she was embracing every opportunity offered to her. Life enhancing perhaps, but more an unexpected last chance for her. Up they went into the canopy of four hundred year old tingle trees, indigenous to Western Australia, as was much of the flora that they were to witness. The climb was gentle, up a ramp of open, diamond patterned galvanised steel walkways, vertical barriers rising each side to above waste height. Dolly glanced down, through the ramp, as they ascended, but decided she'd prefer to look ahead. Betsy strode forward and was in the canopy well before her friend. Andrew remained with his mother, offering words of encouragement to egg her on. The same metallic construction continued, the ground visible below them through the deck, as they stepped along a walkway, strung on poles by steel cables. They swung in the light breeze, the movement of people causing further rocking. Dolly held tightly onto the side-railing. Stopping at a viewing point, she caught her breath and took out her camera to capture the moment. Andrew explained that they were viewing ancient plant life, in existence since Australia was part of the super-continent, Gondwana, before it split to form the current land masses of earth. Dolly listened politely but, what she wanted most, was to descend.

~

Chapter 2 – Spring to Summer

"What was he thinking of?" Diane had arrived and listened to Betsy and Dolly describe their outings since their visit commenced. Bewilderment, consternation and then alarm were her dominant emotions as their story unfolded. The following morning Diane reproached her brother.

"They enjoyed it, well Betsy did. Mum was glad to come down from the canopy, I think."

"They're in their seventies, for Pete's sake," said Diane, her pointed face portraying disgust easily.

"But not dead yet! Anyhow, they're in good shape for their age."

"I knew I should have travelled earlier. I can't trust you to look after them properly."

"For God's sake, Diane, they've had a good time. Do they look miserable?"

Tension crystallised between them and the air developed a frosty hue, tangible to Dolly as she entered the room. She glanced around at her two children peering at Andrew and then at Diane. "Are you two squabbling?"

John entered at the same time as Betsy and they stole a glance at each other, John nodding imperceptibly towards her. "Weekend's here," he said, "I thought we'd have lunch down by the beach. I know just the place."

The thaw began and diplomacy, spearheaded by Dolly and John, began to mend the fences. Betsy made coffee in an effort to provide further lubrication. Later, Dolly whispered to Betsy, "She always was a bossy madam."

Chapter 2 – Spring to Summer

May

The time was passing quickly and sightseeing intensified with Diane's arrival. She was more dynamic in her efforts than Andrew had been and that irony was lost on her. Every tourist attraction around Perth was visited: beaches, along the swan river, a further visit to Kings Park, without incident this time, the zoo, offshore islands, surrounding countryside, shopping precincts and more. The wedding of Andrew and John was imminent too. Andrew, John and Diane organised an Australian speciality, a barbecue, in the evening of the day that Dolly's grandchildren arrived with their father, Danny. Diane arranged a hair appointment for herself, her mother and Betsy for that morning. Betsy tried to exempt herself but Diane ignored her protestations. Resistance evaporated when Betsy discovered that Diane was footing the bill. After their pamper session, Dolly grinned all of the way home; she'd never witnessed her friend with styled hair and was convinced that Betsy was delighted. As evidence, Betsy's head scarf made no appearance that day. Danny's arrival, with grandchildren Timmy, aged twelve, and Joanne, fourteen, started off the celebrations. Dolly noticed that Danny had gained weight, having a prominent paunch, hair was starting to thin and he was greying. His appearance contrasted sharply with the athletic Diane, now restored to blond, with not a hint of grey, thanks to the expertise of the hairdresser. Betsy had met the family when they visited Dolly, some time prior. She could not contain her normal Yorkshire bluntness. "My Timmy and Joanne, how you have grown," she said, predictably, adding, "and so have you Danny. Where's the lithe figure gone?"

Chapter 2 – Spring to Summer

"Ah, it was never lithe," said Diane.

"I see you don't change, Betsy," said Danny, laughing.

Danny was dispatched, with Dolly, Betsy and the grandchildren, to the beach so that the barbecue could be prepared and Dolly took the opportunity to reconnect with her grandchildren, quite changed since the last time she'd been with them. From her video calls, she knew that the children had grown but it hadn't prepared her for such a transformation. Their father had altered too: tolerant, mellow and agreeable, complementing his wife's spiky personality. Later, Danny glanced at his watch and turned to Dolly. "Looks like we've done our time, mum. Time to head back, I think. You hungry? I could eat."

Dolly, smiled looked at Betsy as she nodded. Danny called to Joanne and Timmy who had been revelling along the beach and they ran towards them. 'Does it get any better than this?' Dolly mused as she gathered her few belongings together and stood, ready for the barbecue evening.

~

"We're all paid up," said Walter, striding towards their plot, enjoying a walk along the canal tow path.

"Fifty quid each," said Harold, "Dora was mad. She raided the money for Scarborough, she told me."

"I hadn't told Elsie," said Bert.

"Eye, but Dora did, didn't she?" said Harold, chuckling.

"I should have guessed! Anyhow, I had enough put by, so I didn't have to go cap-in-hand to her."

Chapter 2 – Spring to Summer

Walter watched his old friends; not for the first time, he was pleased that he hadn't married. He'd visited the town clerk and paid their dues for the allotment. They were free of debt and could enter the Allotment Growers' Championship competition, the premier one of the year. The season was progressing, sun higher in the sky and the soil warm. Cloches were off the vegetables, needing little protection now, and the men's precious carrots were growing well, feathery leaves large and healthy. Whether they succumbed to the dastardly carrot fly would not be known until they were lifted; to attempt that, or thin the crop, would invite the critters in, to be avoided at all costs. Their work was paying off: healthy crops, growing well, feeding, watering and weed control their priority.

"I see the lass' opened up the poly tunnel," said Bert, pointing at Beatrice and Ambrose's plot.

"It'll be hot in there during the day," said Walter.

"Let's go and have butchers," said Harold.

"I'm game if you are," said Bert.

The three pensioners sauntered over to number thirty, Bert with his hands deep in his trousers, held up with braces. Standing on the grass path, they peered through the tunnel door straight into the eyes of Beatrice who was feeding and soaking a row of vegetables. She was bending over and straightened as she spotted the men. "Weighing up the competition are you?" said Beatrice, putting down the watering can.

"Not at all," said Walter but the deception in his eyes was clear.

Chapter 2 – Spring to Summer

"How is it all going?" said Harold, jumping in quickly, "Just being neighbourly, Saw you were here, an' all."

Beatrice, face stern, sniffed as she said, "All is well, thank you. This greenhouse has been a Godsend. I don't know what we would have done without it, especially when my carrots were vandalised."

"Vandalised, you think so? Your husband not here?" said Harold, deflecting the conversation away to one more comfortable.

"Ambrose is away today. He still has a little business, in town. Your crops look well, but there's a long time to go until July."

"Oh, we'll be ready for then, we always are," said Bert, smiling.

"Before you go," said Beatrice, the implication obvious, "I have proposed a change to the competition rules for next season, they can't apply for this one as it has started, of course. I hope I can count on your support?"

"What changes are these?" said Harold, glancing at his comrades.

"I think we should move with the times, encourage a more environmental approach, green if you wish. I have proposed to the committee, and a majority have agreed with my recommendation, that competitors should adhere to strict ecological standards, as a condition of entering. We should free our allotments of harmful chemicals, don't you agree?"

~

Chapter 2 – Spring to Summer

The barbecue held a surprise. Andrew invited some of his clients, and one, with his wife, had become a friend, as customers often did. It was Betsy who spotted him first and Dolly was alerted by her exclamation. "My, what are you doing here?"

"Do you know each other?" said Andrew, puzzled.

"We met briefly, in Mandurah," said Jimmy, "We had tea aboard the yacht."

Jimmy and Babs greeted Dolly and Betsy. They told Andrew that they'd recognised them from the TV appearance, after the hullabaloo of Kings Park. Andrew nodded his head, knowingly. The ladies had mentioned meeting the boat owner and his wife to Andrew, but had spared the detail, an exuberance of events occurring with intricacies lost in the telling. "It's a small world," said Dolly.

"It appears to be," replied Babs.

"I've been thinking, about that cruise," said Dolly, addressing Jimmy. She told him about the theft of Catherine's handbag, surprised to discover that Jimmy hadn't known of it, nor of the recovery of Catherine's and another one.

"You're telling me that Alastair may have recovered my bag?" said Jimmy.

"Yes and no," said Betsy.

A perplexed look drifted across Jimmy's face as Dolly butted in, "He was angry about the mugging and chucked the bag into the Med. He thought he was slighting the thief."

"You build up my hopes only to shatter them," said Jimmy.

Chapter 2 – Spring to Summer

Next, Dolly explained about the break-ins, telling the yacht owner that only those who'd been on the cruise had been targeted. Jimmy looked uncomfortable as the narrative unfolded and Babs's mouth dropped open. There was an awkward silence for a moment that seemed longer, broken by Jimmy who beckoned to Andrew. Andrew, glass of red wine in hand, ambled over, smiling, his countenance changing as he sensed the sombre atmosphere. Jimmy thanked Andrew for the invitation to the barbecue, and explained that he and Babs needed to leave. Taking Andrew by the arm, he led him away into a corner and they spoke, Andrew glancing over to his mum intermittently. Jimmy waved at Babs, who bid the ladies goodbye, walking over to join her husband. As Jimmy and Babs left, Andrew strode over to his mother, his visage difficult to read. "I hope we haven't caused you any trouble," said Dolly.

"No, he's always been a difficult client. He wants me to go to his office in Perth tomorrow. I think you need to fill me in on a few details before I go, but not tonight, eh? Let's get this barbecue going, this is meant to be a party, not a wake."

~

"Thank you for coming," said Jimmy, dressed in casual business apparel, deep blue trousers, a white short-sleeved shirt and black brogues, as he welcomed Andrew into his spacious first floor office, overlooking the Swan River. Jimmy's personal assistant, Carter, a tall, smartly dressed, handsome and intelligent young man, brought Andrew a coffee and left, closing the door behind him. Dolly had described to Andrew

Chapter 2 – Spring to Summer

their discourse with Jimmy and Babs on the yacht, and at the barbecue of the previous evening. He was none the wiser, wondering why such minor revelations had caused distress, forcing Jimmy and Babs to abandon the party. Andrew said nothing after their initial greeting. Seated in an armchair, his host opposite across a low table, he waited for Jimmy to explain.

"It's a bit of a mess," he started.

Andrew sipped at his coffee, leaving biscuits on a plate untouched. He remained silent, using the vacuum created to his advantage. "I'd like your advice," said Jimmy.

Andrew leaned forward, replacing his mug on a coaster on the glass topped table. "Is that as a friend, or in my professional capacity as your lawyer?"

"It had better be the latter," said Jimmy, smiling, "and I'll pay your fees."

Jimmy explained that he had something of value that he'd stashed away in a safe, in one of his company buildings. He'd told Dolly and Betsy about a key, but he'd told a white lie: the safe wasn't at a bank. There was only one key, and it had been in his travel bag, which was stolen during their stop in Mallorca.

"What's in the safe. I need to know, if I'm to help," said Andrew, "If it's yours, why can't you have it opened, force it if necessary?"

Chapter 2 – Spring to Summer

"I can't share the contents, Andrew. What I can tell you is that it's a historical artefact, priceless, and I don't want its identity or whereabouts known. You'll have to trust me on this."

"Is that why you don't want a locksmith to open it?"

"Andrew, it's protected. There's a chance that a forced opening would destroy the contents. Maybe I was foolish, having a single key. Seemed a sound strategy at the time."

"Hindsight is good sight, Jimmy. So, what do you want from me?"

Jimmy glanced out of the window down at the Swan River, as he considered his next move. "I've been a bit heavy handed," he said, staring into Andrew's eyes.

Jimmy explained that he'd employed a private investigator to find and retrieve the key. He'd told them to start in Mallorca and pursue the trail to wherever it led. The route snaked to Heythwaite, and his companions on the cruise. "I gave them a free hand, Andrew."

"It looks like they've taken you literally. There are laws, Jimmy. If this finds its way back to you …"

"It will be bad, I know," said Jimmy, completing Andrew's assertion.

"I'm a solicitor, Jimmy. I can only act within the law."

"I'm not asking you to do anything dishonest," said Jimmy, "Go through the paperwork, prove they were acting on their own, outside of my brief."

Andrew nodded and said, "Okay, when do I start?"

Chapter 2 – Spring to Summer

"No time like the present, hey? Carter, my PA, will furnish you with the files. Do what you can."

Jimmy instructed Andrew to examine the contract between the investigator and Jimmy's firm, to make sure it was water tight and make amends where he found gaps. Andrew knew what was required; he was walking a fine line. "I'm sorry I left in a hurry yesterday. Something came up," said Jimmy, as he closed the door, leaving Andrew with Carter.

~

Amy was feeding her son, now named Kit, the closest male name they could match with Catherine, his deceased grandmother. Alastair, seated in his armchair, smiled, delighted with the new addition. In stocking feet, Robert walked in from the kitchen, leaving his boots by the side entrance. He'd been in the fields with the agronomist; the crops were growing, weather now pleasant. The next task was a feed and he wanted to be sure that the nutrients supplied were the right quantity, hence the agronomist. Money well spent, he thought, though his father was old school, preferring a seat of the pants approach.

"I've checked on the sheep," said Alastair, "No need to do that." Alastair usually tended his Wensleydale's, as he called them. They were his pride and joy and he was pleased to see the lambs jumping in the fields in the late spring weather. Robert smiled at his dad, leaned over to plant a kiss on his son's head and a peck on his wife's cheek.

"Sit down lad, will you," said Alastair, "I've something to say."

Chapter 2 – Spring to Summer

Robert glanced at Amy as he sat on the sofa next to her. "What is it dad, you look serious."

Alastair was holding a brown envelope. He placed his hand inside and pulled out a black rectangular object, rather like a key fob, but without any key. He handed it to Robert who placed it in the palm of his hand to examine it. "What is it?"

"I'm not sure," said Alastair, "It was in that bag that I threw into the Med. I kept it, didn't want to chuck it."

Robert looked at Amy as he said, "Is this what they were hoping to find, during the break-ins, I mean?"

"They didn't because it was in the tractor, with me," said Alastair, "To be honest with you, I'd forgotten all about it, until the break-in, then I put two and two together."

"You didn't think to mention it?" said Amy.

"You had enough on your plate, love," said Alastair.

"You know what it reminds me of?" said Robert.

Amy glanced at Alastair, but they both remained mute, so Robert continued, "One of those keyless locks you find in newer cars."

"I wonder what it opens," said Amy.

"Sixty four million dollar question, that is," said Alastair.

~

Jimmy and Babs came to the wedding of Andrew and John, staying until the end. The atmosphere was charged the whole day and the company abundant and convivial. Dolly, mother of the groom, revelled in her role, socialising as if her life

Chapter 2 – Spring to Summer

depended upon it. John asked Betsy to escort him down the isle; his mother had died when he was young and he'd developed a bond with the cantankerous Yorkshire lass since she'd arrived. Astonished at being asked, Betsy bought a new frock for the occasion, frequenting the hairdresser again for the second time in two decades. Joanne, Dolly's granddaughter, applied the make-up. The result was a radiant Betsy, arm in arm with John as they marched, military style, towards Andrew. Cheshire cat smiles decorated both of their faces and, as they reached Andrew, John pecked Betsy on her cheek and escorted her to the chair, next to Dolly, before joining his partner. Elation remained with Betsy for the rest of the celebration. Guests started to drift away in the evening from eleven o'clock onwards, after John and Andrew had left for the airport hotel, their honeymoon flight being early the following morning. Janet, Betsy and Dolly retired to the main lounge, each with a mug of steaming tea. "It's been lovely," said Dolly.

"May we join you," said a voice from behind, recognisable as Jimmy's. They'd seen Babs and Jimmy during the hectic day with little opportunity to chat and had no contact with them since the barbecue. Andrew had been circumspect about his meeting with Jimmy, merely saying that it was 'about business'.

"You'll be leaving soon, I hear," said Babs.

"Two more days, that's all. It's gone quickly," said Betsy.

"Too quickly," said Dolly.

They spoke about the day, how pleasant it had been, and how delighted they were that Andrew and John were able to tie the

Chapter 2 – Spring to Summer

knot. Babs asked about Dolly and Betsy's holiday in Australia, polite conversation to fill time. Then, the uncomfortable moment came and it was time for Jimmy and Babs to leave. Jimmy stood first and his wife followed him. Dolly escorted them to the door, and the awaiting transport shuttle arranged by her son. "I wanted to say sorry," said Jimmy as they stood at the doorway.

"What about?" said Dolly.

"Leaving the barbecue early," said Babs, butting in, glancing at her husband, "Come on Jimmy, the man's waiting. Have a safe journey home. When you come back, look us up."

Jimmy hesitated as Babs scurried to the car. Turning towards Dolly, a look of contrition in his eyes, he kissed her cheek, saying, "Pass on my regards to my cruising companions, and regret for what they have suffered."

He turned slowly and walked towards Babs, without looking over his shoulder. Dolly returned to the lounge and Diane had joined Janet and Betsy on the couch. "Are you alright, Dolly?" said Janet, noticing the preoccupied mien of her friend's face.

Dolly pulled another chair close, lowering herself into it as Betsy pushed the mug of tea closer to her. Diane became concerned. "Mum, has something happened?"

"Nothing to worry about, dear. Those people are odd. I'm sure he was trying to tell me something, but I don't know what."

Chapter 2 – Spring to Summer

"Jimmy and Babs?" said Janet, then continued, "They talk in riddles, if you ask me. Don't you go worrying yourself and don't let it spoil a fantastic day."

Dolly's smile returned to her face, dimples showing again, as she said, "Yes, it has been and one I'll always remember."

~

"How's the allotment going, Uncle Bert? Going to win those trophies this year?" said Daniel. Daniel's grandfather was a good friend of Bert, the reason that Daniel addressed Bert as his uncle, an honorary title. Daniel had returned home from his day's work, dropped off near the Co-operative store so that he could buy a soft drink before he walked home.

"Going well, lad. Can't let that stuck-up woman win any," Bert said, chuckling.

"Seems to be involved in everything, that one. I hear she's standing for the Town Council at the elections. Don't know where she finds the time."

"Is she now?" said Bert.

"So grandad told me," said Daniel.

Bert pondered as Daniel took a swig of his drink from the bottle and decided to change the conversation flow, "You finishing soon, the apprenticeship, I mean?"

"End of June, can't wait to be qualified. More money would be good."

"You're dating Angie now, aren't you?"

Chapter 2 – Spring to Summer

Daniel smiled at Bert's outmoded language, "We're hanging out, yes."

"I can see why you need more money," Bert said, laughing.

"Got to go, uncle," said Daniel, not wishing to discuss his romantic attachments, "Mum will have tea ready. I sent her a text just as the van came in to Heythwaite."

"Okay, lad, see you around."

Bert headed for Harold's house, opposite the empty home of Betsy. Dora was taking care of it while Betsy was away and was cleaning the windows as Bert arrived. She told him that Harold was 'out back', meaning that he was tending their tiny garden. He walked into the terraced house, through the kitchen and out of the rear door. Harold was dead-heading late flowering bulbs to allow the plants to concentrate on bulking up for the next year's floral tribute. They exchanged views on the season's flush of flowers and the coming summer, flaunting its delights, still out of reach. He wanted to broach the subject of 'chemicals' with Harold. They'd accumulated them, hoarding concoctions before a ban came into effect. "We rely on them, Harold. I've just treated the leeks."

Bert had detected the start of the rust fungus on their leeks, the weather having been inclement recently after an early period of warmth encouraging the blight. He'd sprayed them with a now illegal fungicide, knowing that it would nip the problem in the bud. "I spoke to Walter," said Bert, "He's put some feelers out."

Chapter 2 – Spring to Summer

Harold stopped snipping and stood to face Bert, saying, "What does he think?"

"He thinks she'll get her way. Most of the committee, and well over half the plot holders, think organic is the way forward. We're out on a limb, Harold."

"Looks like we've got to accept it, Bert."

Bert told Harold about his chance meeting with Daniel, informing him of the news about Beatrice standing for the Town Council. Harold shook his head, wondering if 'that woman' was going to run every organ of Heythwaite. "Dora will be furious. She's already mad about her being on the Allotment Growers' Association committee. She blames us for letting her in."

"We couldn't stop her," said Bert, "She was voted on, fair and democratic."

"That's not what Dora thinks."

"That's as well as might be," said Bert, "I have an idea. Walter's well known around here. Suppose we persuaded him to stand? You think he would?"

"He'd likely have more support than she would. It's worth a try, Bert." Dora came into the garden and Bert winked at Harold, mouthing that he would approach Walter. Harold nodded, in agreement.

"Hasn't he offered you any tea, yet. You two can gossip for Yorkshire. I've got cake," said Dora, ducking back into the house.

~

105

Chapter 2 – Spring to Summer

"I hear they're back," said Ambrose, "That feisty woman, Betsy and her jolly friend, Dolly." Beatrice and Ambrose were also dead-heading in their considerable garden, easily the largest in the Pastures, 'A place to set roots' as the marketing people remarked when they viewed their home before purchasing it. After snipping off the dead flowers, Beatrice doubled over the leaves and bound them with green hemp twine, a practice derided by horticulturalists; Beatrice considered it 'tidier' and it allowed the tulips to excel, flowering in succession to the daffodils.

"I should think they're tired after that flight. When did they arrive?"

"Yesterday, but they haven't been seen since Edwina dropped them off," said Ambrose.

"I didn't realise they were friends with the café owner."

"A funny relationship, but somehow it works. They'll be adjusting after the jet lag. It is pretty awful, especially at their age."

"At any age, dear."

Ambrose was managing Beatrice's campaign for election to the Town Council. He'd studied the regulations, especially the spending limits, which were strict. All expenditure had to be recorded and he was meticulous in his bookkeeping. An unexpected candidate, Walter, the allotment holder, had entered the campaign. His canvassing was amateur by comparison, and his spending negligible, but Ambrose knew that he was popular. Emphasising the negative in an opponent would be

Chapter 2 – Spring to Summer

bad form in Heythwaite, something to be avoided, for it would not be forgiven; they had to live in the community, a cross that most Westminster politicians didn't carry. The elections would be held towards the end of June, which was nearly five weeks away. Plenty of time to sway hearts and minds, thought Ambrose.

~

"Dora says they're home," said Harold, "Arrived yesterday. Nobody's seen them yet." The sun was high but the wind was cold so the three plot holders were seated around their paraffin stove in the wooden shed. Summer was over the horizon but spring reminded them that it could still bite and they knew that the cold spell would arrest the growth of their plants, now protected again by cloches, especially those for the competition.

"Be catching up with their sleep," said Walter, scratching the side of his head as he handed a packet of chocolate finger biscuits to Bert. They'd talked about the election campaign. Dora had seen Beatrice's posters throughout the town, prominent in many shop windows. She was popular with the High Street traders, being a big spender in many of the stores. Dora had hounded Harold, wanting to know 'what Walter was going to do because he *had* to win'. Walter was sanguine about his campaign; he'd lived in Heythwaite all of his life and was known by most residents. He often walked the high street, chatting to folk as they passed. Few mentioned the election but he *knew* that their support was guaranteed. He didn't need

Chapter 2 – Spring to Summer

fancy posters; after all, this was a Town Council election, not a parliamentary one.

"Did Dora speak to them?" said Bert, "Did they have a good time?"

Harold explained that Dora had been cleaning her windows when Edwina arrived with her charge, having dropped Dolly in the High Street. Walter glanced at Bert, both knowing that there was little that happened in Heythwaite that passed Dora by. Betsy was inside her house before Dora managed to reach her front door, so there was no chance to ask any questions. "All in good time," said Walter, "I'm sure we'll find out what happened on their adventure."

~

Dolly had popped round to see Betsy to check how she was feeling. Dolly felt like she'd been drugged. Her rhythms lacked synchronisation, waking at odd times, hungry at others and her bowel movements, well they were peculiar. She spotted Dora at the window and waved but managed to pop inside Betsy's before Dora made an appearance. She couldn't face an interrogation from Harold's wife that day. Betsy looked pale and drawn, causing Dolly to ask, "Are you alright, dear. You don't look it."

"I've just woken," said Betsy, "I seem to want to sleep when I should be awake and be awake when I should be sleeping."

"It's awful, isn't it?"

"How long does it last?"

"A few days," said Betsy, "Each day will be better."

Chapter 2 – Spring to Summer

"I'll make a cuppa," said Betsy.

"Sounds lovely, dear."

Dolly followed Betsy through to the kitchenette, seating herself in her usual chair as Betsy filled the kettle, lit the gas hob and placed the utensil on to boil. "Have you had breakfast?" said Betsy, "Dora left me some bread, butter and milk. I could make some toast. I've some jam unopened too."

"That would be nice," said Dolly, "I avoided her this morning. I shouldn't have been so nasty."

"There's not a mean bone in your body Dolly Jackson. There's a time and place for the likes of Dora. We'll face her when this passes, eh?"

Dolly smiled as she watched Betsy open the loaf of sliced bread and place four pieces in the toaster. "Did you enjoy the trip, Betsy?"

Betsy turned to Dolly, tears welling up in eyes that hadn't seen moisture like it in decades, and said, "The best, Dolly."

June

May, in like a lion, out like a lamb, more normal for March, the proverb predicts. Finally, with longer days, the hint of summer warmth to come had become stronger. The earth bathed in it, stirring it with the April and May rains, repeating the miracle of expanding flora. Bert was alone on the allotment and had removed the protective cloches. Yawning, he seemed perpetually tired these days. The carrots had recovered their vigour, bushy leaves half way up the fence erected to shield them from their individual pest, the carrot fly. His illicit

Chapter 2 – Spring to Summer

spraying had nipped the rust fungus in the bud and the rest of the plants appeared to be healthy. Continual weeding was the task, reducing competition so that their crops received the best. Bert leaned on his Dutch hoe, to rest from his labour. Looking up he spotted Ambrose, striding towards his plot. Ambrose lifted his hand in greeting and Bert returned the gesture reluctantly, unable to avoid some social interaction. Ambrose, changed direction, stopping at the edge of the allotment adjacent to Bert's. "Grand morning, Bert," he yelled so that Bert could hear.

"It is that, Ambrose. Nice to be out here. How's it all going?"

They exchanged views about the weather and the growing season, but avoided the upcoming competition. As Ambrose walked away, Bert watched him and said to himself, in a low voice, "He's not a bad lad. If circumstances were different ..."

Bert left the thought floating for he knew that, with Beatrice the dominant force, the best they could expect was politeness. He returned to his hoeing and let his thoughts drift to the conversation he'd had with Dolly, catching up on their trip down-under. Dolly had been surprised that their 'little episode in Kings Park', as she put it, had made the news in the UK. She went on to tell Bert how the event had opened some doors, especially how they'd met Jimmy and Babs. Bert had listened with incredulity as the story unfolded: the Australians being on the same cruise as those from Heythwaite, Jimmy being a client of her son's and Alastair recovering Jimmy's bag, but not knowing it. She'd finished by telling Bert that something had unsettled Jimmy at Andrew's barbecue and she still wasn't sure

Chapter 2 – Spring to Summer

what it was. All very Agatha Christie, thought Bert but his deliberations were interrupted by the arrival of Walter.

"Penny for them, lad."

"Walter," said Bert, "Yes, I was miles away, wasn't I? I was thinking about Dolly."

"Don't let Elsie know," said Walter, smiling.

"Bert grinned as he said, "As if, no, what she told me about that guy who was on the cruise with Alastair's crew."

"A rum do, for sure," said Walter, "Fancy a cuppa? It looks like you've been here a while."

"Grand, I'll just finish this row."

"I'll go and make it. Then, I'll start the other end. Maybe we'll meet in the middle?"

~

Angie had straightened hair, almost black with a hint of red, and wore it at her shoulders. She dressed smartly, business like, in dark two piece suits, sometimes complemented with a skirt, sometimes with trousers. She was a recent graduate, finishing a part-time degree with help from her employer, a global communications company. She was employed as an engineer, hoping to be Chartered one day, and already a member of the biggest engineering institution in the UK. She'd studied at Leeds Metropolitan University, attending one day a week, plus two evenings and an annual summer school. It had allowed her to achieve a degree without running up huge debts, and earn a salary at the same time. It took longer but the work and life experience was something that she would never have achieved

Chapter 2 – Spring to Summer

if she'd traversed a conventional route. Convention wasn't something that bothered Angie. She ploughed her own furrow, that was her way. Daniel and Angie knew of each other, in Heythwaite everyone knew everyone else, but neither had considered the other as partners until a chance meeting at the library in Skipton. Both of them wanted peace and quiet, Daniel to complete an assignment for his electrical college course and Angie to do some network design. They acknowledged each other, but kept their distance, except that Angie had noticed Daniel glancing over at her and smiling. She'd nodded in return. They met for coffee afterwards, discovered that they had much in common, and that's how the relationship started. Angie worked throughout Yorkshire, and surrounding counties, helping build communications infrastructure for the corporations that made their home there. She was based in Leeds, taking the train, a local bus delivering her to the railway station in Skipton. Considering the distance, the journey, like her day, was long. She was learning to drive, hoping to pass her test soon. She'd achieved success in the theory test so was ready for the main chance. However, parking in Leeds was difficult and expensive, so she feared that she'd be stuck with public transport for the foreseeable future. Waiting at the side of the road for her instructor to arrive, a van emblazoned with 'Yorkshire's Premier Electrical Contractor' turned the corner, stopped in front of her and a beaming Daniel leapt out. He said 'cheerio' to his workmate, slammed the door and gave Angie a kiss in greeting. "I was hoping I'd see you," said Daniel as the van drove away, "I knew it was one of your driving lessons this evening."

Chapter 2 – Spring to Summer

"You look a bit mucky."

"First fixing. Hacking out stone walls, some of them pretty solid," said Daniel.

"I was working from home, well the library. Too much going on at home. We've a network going in next week, in Ilkley, pretty easy, finished the design today."

"You're lucky you can do that, work from home I mean."

"Yes, suppose putting circuits in means you have to be there," Angie said smiling, "What's up? Why did you want to meet up?"

"It's always great to see you," said Daniel.

"Charmer," said Angie, glancing into Daniel's eyes, disturbing his karma.

At that point, the farmer Alastair wandered past heading down the high street. Both Daniel and Angie acknowledged him, but he didn't stop. "He seemed in a hurry. Anyhow, I need a favour."

As Daniel spoke the words, a Citroën C3, sporting the logo 'Tony Parkinson, Driving Instructor, 90% Pass First Time' turned the corner and screeched to a halt in front of the couple. The middle aged man, hair speckled with grey, waved his hand.

"Sandpiper, eight o'clock, we'll talk then," said Angie.

The instructor stepped from the car as Angie walked to the driver's side, seated herself in front of the steering wheel, adjusted the chair, mirror and attached her belt. Daniel watched, the instructor seated beside Angie, as she glanced in

Chapter 2 – Spring to Summer

the mirror, indicated, took a final look over her shoulder and drove gently down the road. He nodded, sure that she'd pass her test easily.

~

Dolly greeted Alastair and showed him through to her kitchen, and then into the conservatory, now open as the weather had improved. Supplied with hot tea and biscuits, Alastair seated across from Dolly, a low coffee table separating them, took a slurp of his coffee. They exchanged news, especially about his grandson, Kit, now well into his third month. "He has a good appetite, fair wearing Amy out."

"Oh, she'll cope and it'll start to get easier for her soon, once she's finished with breast feeding. Special times, Alastair, they pass so quickly," said Dolly.

"That they do, lass, that they do."

Alastair was pensive for a moment and Dolly, perceptive that he wanted to say something, placed her cup and saucer on the glass topped table and leaned forward. "It's about the trip," said Alastair, reaching into his tweed jacket pocket.

"I thought it might be," said Dolly, smiling.

"Amy told me, what happened in Australia, you meeting Jimmy and Babs. Right odd, what a coincidence. Beyond belief, love, like in a novel." Alastair opened his left hand to reveal a rectangular black object, a couple of buttons embedded in one side as he said, "I think this is what that chap was looking for."

Chapter 2 – Spring to Summer

Dolly glanced at the fob and nodded, "Was that in the bag you found?"

"It was. I'd forgotten about it, well mostly, until the break-ins. It didn't seem right to chuck it. I thought it was for a car. If someone had mentioned they'd lost it, on the cruise I mean, I'd have handed it in."

"It is what it is, Alastair. Would you like me to show it to Jimmy, he's the man I met in in Perth, the one on your cruise?"

"How you going to do that? You're not going back are you?"

"Not for a while, dear. It takes it out of you. I've only just got over the last trip. I can use my tablet to make a call to Andrew. Jimmy's a client of his."

"Beyond me," said Alastair, glancing at the device as Dolly showed it to him, "Robert will know. Everyone I love is right with me."

"You're lucky," said Dolly as she watched Alastair's countenance change.

"Pity Catherine didn't see the nipper. He's full of life and a right porker." Alastair attempted a smile, finished his tea and stood, ready to leave, saying, "Can I leave that with you, Dolly? Send it to him if you think it's right. I'll pay the postage."

"Yes, Alastair. I'll let you know what they want me to do. I'll not do anything without asking you first."

~

Chapter 2 – Spring to Summer

"Spritzer is it?" said Daniel, as Angie entered the Sandpiper bar.

"Wine, red, I think," said Angie, "Just a small one."

"Was the driving lesson that bad?"

"Cheeky, no it went well. Parallel parking, reversing round corners and town driving. He's a good instructor."

Daniel returned from the bar with a glass of Merlot for Angie and a pint of Theakston's best bitter for himself. "So, what was this favour?" said Angie, sipping her wine.

"It's Uncle Bert," said Daniel.

"I don't know anything about growing plants!"

"No, it's not that. He's worried that Walter isn't doing enough about the election for the Town Council. He wants some posters and leaflets producing. Bert's worried. He thinks that woman from the Pastures might win."

"Well, she might," said Angie, "Especially if Walter isn't prepared to put in the effort. She'll deserve to win."

"You think?" said Daniel, "She's a bit stuck-up isn't she?"

"She's a woman who knows what she wants. Done a lot to shake up things round here. We could do with more like her, if you ask me."

Daniel glanced at Angie. He'd misjudged her; the response wasn't what he'd expected.

"Anyhow, what was the favour, and don't say you wanted me to do the posters, because the answer's no. If Walter can't get off his backside and try to win, then he doesn't deserve to be a

Chapter 2 – Spring to Summer

Town Councillor." Angie stared at Daniel and laughed as she said, "You were, you were going to ask me to prepare leaflets."

"Well, yes I was, but you've swayed me and you're right. If Walter wants the election, he'll have to work for it. Now, how about you?"

"What about me?"

"You stand. We could do with new blood on that council. It's full of old geezers, and Beatrice isn't much younger."

"Yes, but at least she's a woman. Anyway, they're the ones with the time," said Angie, "You can't be serious Dan."

"Deadly serious Angie. Is there still time to register?"

Angie looked into Daniel's eyes; his idea was starting to stir some interest within her. She paused for a moment before saying. "I don't know, but I'll find out. You're on Dan."

~

Ambrose and Beatrice had finished their hoeing, standing at the end of the allotment, near the compost heaps. The sun was warm and there was a light breeze on a pleasant day. They'd been discussing a new entrant to the Town Council elections, a young woman called Angie. She was a late runner, registering with a few hours to go before nominations closed. Her appearance had added a spark to the fire. Within days of throwing her glove into the ring, she'd drawn up a manifesto, posters had appeared throughout the town and a professional leaflet had been dropped through each letterbox of Heythwaite. Angie had booked the village hall on two occasions and held public meetings intending to be the 'listening voice of

Heythwaite'. She was proving to be popular, her youth an advantage, her competence on the hustings outweighing her apparent inexperience. "She's more of a challenge than the old guy, Walter," said Ambrose.

"You don't think I know that, dear," said Beatrice.

"She's young too."

"That just means she's green," said Beatrice.

"She's good in public."

"Are you trying to help?" said Beatrice.

"You need to know your adversary. You want to win, don't you?" said Ambrose.

"I know that tone. You have an idea?"

"Who is it that turns out and votes?"

"Older electorates," said Beatrice, "Oh, I see. Angie will be more attractive to the younger voters. I should appeal to the more mature among us."

"Exactly, pitch the campaign towards the middle aged and elderly. Angie has an uphill struggle if she wants the young to turn out, let alone vote for her."

"You're a genius, Ambrose. I know exactly what I should do."

~

Walter put his glass down on the table, fingering it as he contemplated. "Spit it out," said Harold, "You've been in an odd mood all evening."

Chapter 2 – Spring to Summer

"Better out than in," said Bert, finishing his pint, "Down that one, lad, and I'll get another round in."

The landlady spotted Bert as he started to rise and shouted, "Save your legs, Bert. Same again is it? I'll bring them over."

"Thanks Nancy," said Bert.

"It's this blasted election, I'm not cut out for it. Angie's in now and she'll win against Beatrice."

"I'm not so sure," said Harold, "She appeals to the youngsters but she's inexperienced. Beatrice might have the edge with the older folk."

"I see what Harold's saying," said Bert, "You might split the old'ns vote, and that would allow Angie to win. She's running a grand campaign, looks competent to me. Our Daniel says she's a lass that knows what she wants."

"Well, he should know," said Walter, his demeanour brightening, "Her problem is getting the youngsters to turn out, they don't usually bother for a Town election."

"No, but us oldies do. That's my point," said Harold, "If you stay in the race, you'll cut down the number who support Beatrice and that might get Angie elected."

"So, I'll have done some good, but won't be on the council," said Walter, "That would suit me just fine."

"Don't give that impression, Walter, or people will think you're not serious."

"Perish the thought," said Walter as Nancy delivered their beers.

Chapter 2 – Spring to Summer

~

Betsy and Dolly were at Skipton market, being Wednesday. Their baskets were full and drizzle had started to fall so they'd taken refuge in a coffee shop on Coach Street, an independent, liked by both women. They'd discussed the Town Council election on the bus trip from Heythwaite but had spent little time on it. They weren't going to support Beatrice, thought that Walter was 'nice but clueless' and rated Angie highly. They'd been to one of her village hall electioneering meetings and were impressed. "That's a lass who's going places," Betsy had said as they'd left the hall.

Betsy had ordered a tea and a cherry bakewell and Dolly was having a scone with butter and jam, plus a filtered coffee with hot milk. As the waitress delivered their order, Betsy asked Dolly a question. "Is it tonight you're speaking to Andrew?"

"I spoke to him this morning, dear. It's more convenient that way, it was four in the afternoon for Andrew."

"Had he spoken to Jimmy?"

"Tomorrow, he's meeting up with him. I'm going to contact him at ten o'clock tomorrow morning, it'll be six o'clock there. I took a few pictures of the key fob and he's sent them to Jimmy already."

"Hasn't he heard back?"

"I don't know, dear, I'll find out tomorrow. Come round if you're doing nothing, you can speak to him too, he'd like that."

"Will John be there?"

Chapter 2 – Spring to Summer

"I expect so," said Dolly, smiling. Betsy's attachment to Andrew's partner had been an unexpected bonus of their visit.

~

It was just after six thirty and Walter had walked the length of Heythwaite, knocking on doors, canvassing. Bert had told him that he needed to be seen around town if he had any chance of taking votes from 'that woman'. Mostly, the reception had been polite, pleasant in some cases, but he left with the feeling that he was simply filling in time. It seemed to him that he wasn't being viewed as a serious candidate. He'd decided to have a meal at 'The Old Oak', making that his last port of call for the evening. Betsy wandered down the hill as he crossed the road. She stopped, waving as she spotted him. "Not down the allotment?" said Betsy, as Walter stepped onto the walkway.

"Drumming up support," said Walter, causing Betsy to screw up her face, incomprehension evident, "The election, for the Town Council."

"Ah, well good luck with that," said Betsy, "You meeting your cronies in the 'Oak'?"

"I'm going to have a bite to eat. Bert usually pops in for one at seven so I might see him." Betsy smiled at Walter and took her leave. He watched as she crossed the High Street and darted down the hill, turning at her road. Since she took her trip to Australia, she'd been different, softer around the edges. His respect for her had grown and part of him was envious that she'd had the pluck to make the journey. As he entered the pub he was still musing on Betsy's adventure.

Chapter 2 – Spring to Summer

"Pie and mash, Nancy, what is it today?" said Walter, standing at the bar.

"Steak and ale, is that okay? Do you want mushy or garden peas?"

"Mushy please, Nancy, and a pint of the usual."

"Be right with you, Walter, take a seat, I'll bring it over."

Walter wandered over to a table near the window, one he, Bert and Harold used regularly. As he seated himself on the bench, nearest the wall, Harold came through the door, acknowledged Walter and caught Nancy's eye, who nodded. He joined Walter at the table. "Betsy said you were here. Didn't want you drinking on your own."

"Dora given you a pass-out?" said Walter, smiling.

Harold grinned as he said, "I think she likes me out from under her feet. Betsy told me you'd been door-to-door. How was it?"

"Fine, spent a lot of time chatting and listening to gripes. Most people were nice, but I'm out of my depth, Harold."

"Not long now, Walter, then we can get back to normal."

"Two weeks, seems like and eternity!"

~

Dolly had her tablet propped upright on the table. She and Betsy were seated in front of it and the image of Andrew and John decorated the screen. Betsy and John had chatted, catching up on Australian and Yorkshire gossip and Andrew

Chapter 2 – Spring to Summer

had cut to the chase, finally discussing the key fob. "Mum, Jimmy was ecstatic. I've never seen him like it."

"Should I send it to him?" said Dolly.

"No! You hold on to it. Jimmy's going to send his PA, be there in a couple of days. The guy's name is Carter. I'll send you his photo. You are not to give the fob to anyone else. Can you look after it until then? Jimmy said that it's very important."

"What's in the safe that this key opens? It must be valuable for him to send someone half way around the world." said Betsy.

"Search me," said Andrew, "Jimmy's not saying."

"This is all legal, dear?" said Dolly.

"I'm a lawyer, mum. I wouldn't do anything that isn't within the law."

John and Betsy exchanged a glance that spanned the miles and she knew that John would find answers to the unspoken question she wanted to ask. As the call ended and the image of Andrew and John faded from the screen, Betsy turned to Dolly, saying, "Peculiar, this whole thing Dolly. How about a cuppa? It might clear the fuzz left in my head after that."

The tablet made a sound.

"What's that?" said Betsy.

"Andrew's sent that photo of Jimmy's PA," said Dolly, leaning forward to retrieve the device and tap the screen to open the photo.

Chapter 2 – Spring to Summer

"My, he's a handsome lad," said Betsy.

"He is, dear, he'll turn some heads around here. I wonder how long he'll stay?"

~

"Spit it out, John," said Andrew as he put his smartphone into sleep mode, "You and Betsy can talk without words, even over that distance. Something's bothering you both."

"I trust you," John started, brushing his hand through his red hair.

"I feel a 'but' coming," said Andrew, staring at his husband.

"It's Jimmy, he's not being completely honest with you," said John, "It doesn't seem that the relationship is balanced.

"John, you know I can't discuss my client's business, not with anyone."

"I'm not seeking that but you need to ask yourself a question: what am I getting into, is there any risk to me?"

"That's two questions," said Andrew, smiling, "What's troubling you is that I don't know what's in that safe, yes?"

John nodded, head lowered, eyes glancing upwards into Andrew's.

"Whatever it is, it might be illegal, is that it?"

"More or less, but I'm more worried that he isn't telling you," said John, "You're his lawyer, for Pete's sake."

"Then I'll ask him, today, before Carter leaves for the UK. Happy?"

Chapter 2 – Spring to Summer

"I'll be happy when you're done with this, Andrew. Jimmy's his own man, he works to his own agenda, you're collateral."

"Collateral?"

"Useful, but not important. That's not how I see you."

Andrew smiled as he said, "I'll be careful, John. I can see that you are looking after my interests."

"So is Betsy!"

"No, mate, It's you that Betsy is looking after, she doesn't want to see you hurt. If she was a bloke, I'd be jealous."

~

Jimmy stood and walked around the desk as Andrew was shown into the office by Carter. Jimmy pointed at two chairs positioned around a low table and they took positions perpendicular to each other. Andrew asked of Babs and they exchanged chit-chat as Carter breezed in with coffee and a plate of Arnott's Tim Tam biscuits. As he closed the door it was Andrew who spoke first. "Dolly, my mother, will take care of the key fob. When will Carter leave?"

"Tomorrow, he's staying in London overnight when he arrives, catch up on his sleep. Then a shuttle up to Leeds airport and hiring a car from there. So, arriving Monday, I'd expect, all being well."

"Where's he staying in Heythwaite?"

"The Old Oak, it's a pub with rooms, he tells me."

"I know it, it's tidy enough. He's returning, when?"

Chapter 2 – Spring to Summer

"I've given him a couple of days to catch his breath, so he'll be back here Friday, with the time difference," said Jimmy, "Is there a problem, Andrew? You are being thorough about my PA's travel arrangements."

"No problem, Jimmy. I'm a solicitor, always meticulous, it goes with the territory."

Jimmy smiled and placed his cup on the table, leaning forward, "There's something else, Andrew, I know you too well. Spill the beans."

Andrew took a sip of his coffee and, mimicking Jimmy, leaned forward too. Linking his fingers together at his lap, he took a deep breath. "Whatever we say to each other goes no further."

"I know that, Andrew."

"We need trust between us."

Jimmy sat back in his chair, raising his hands as he replied, "There is! What's your problem, let's get to the point shall we?"

"I need to know what's in that safe, and before Carter leaves."

The atmosphere turned icy as Andrew and Jimmy glared at each other. Finally, Jimmy picked up his cup, took a sip of the warm coffee, cradled the mug in his hands before returning it to the table. "On this you need to have faith in me, Andrew."

"I do, Jimmy. What I need is certainty."

Chapter 2 – Spring to Summer

"Certainty? This isn't about identity is it? You don't care what's in the safe, really. It's about whether what we're doing is legal or not, is that right?"

"Yes, Jimmy. You wouldn't expect me to cooperate otherwise, would you?"

Jimmy paused. Andrew's use of the word 'cooperate' had disturbed him. Andrew held all of the cards: his mother had the key fob. Andrew had been Jimmy's legal counsel for a long time, rarely challenging him in the manner of today, robust but never confrontational. This day was different and Jimmy knew that Andrew meant business. "I think I understand," said Jimmy, finally, breaking the chill.

Andrew nodded but said nothing. "Integrity, that's what's troubling you. Not mine, but yours."

Again, Andrew nodded, smiling weakly this time. "Okay, Andrew, I'll meet you half way. I give you my word that nothing we are doing is illegal, is that enough?"

The two men stared at each other, the silence overwhelming. "I see that it isn't," said Jimmy, "In your eyes I detect 'why doesn't he trust me', the unspoken question. We go back a long way, Andrew. I don't want this small thing to sour our relationship."

Andrew was considering his options and knew that Jimmy didn't wish to disclose the contents of the safe. He made his decision. "Of course I accept your word, Jimmy, but let's have it in writing shall we? I am a lawyer, after all."

Chapter 2 – Spring to Summer

Jimmy smiled and stood, stretching out his hand as Andrew did the same. They shook on the deal and Jimmy called to Carter, who drew up an agreement between the two men, puzzled by its concise content. "When you're in England, say hello to mum for me, Carter."

"Sure," said Carter, grinning.

~

The Town Council election came, merged with those of the Borough and County. It wasn't like the general election, where candidates, standing solemnly on a podium, awaited the results that would determine their fate. The Town's results were counted last, the low voter turnout determined by the bigger elections rather than interest within the town. Before leaving for work, Angie checked the internet for the results but there were none shown. At lunch she checked again: Walter had gained ten votes and Beatrice was the same number of votes ahead of her. A recount had been ordered and was in progress, with the final count expected by the evening. Within the 'Pastures' estate, Beatrice had examined the election web site, disappointed that she hadn't won decisively. Angie had been a formidable adversary and had gained Beatrice's admiration. Beatrice played to win; even a small margin was enough. She smiled as she studied the results, pleased that Walter had done so poorly. She'd reckoned that the votes he'd received were from his allotment friends and their family; they were unlikely to have voted for her so he'd succeeded in reducing Angie's vote. Harold wandered round to Walter's house after his wife told him of the results at lunch time. The recount would make

Chapter 2 – Spring to Summer

no difference to Walter's standing in the election and Walter wasn't internet savvy so was unaware of his position. When Harold told him that he'd received ten votes, Walter put his hands up to his face, a look of shock drifting across it. A mixture of emotions circulated: embarrassment that few had supported him, pleasure at not being elected and annoyance that he'd wasted so much time. Harold made a cup of tea as compensation, to accompany the chocolate digestives he'd brought, because he knew that they'd be needed. By the evening, the recount was finished and it complicated matters. It discovered twelve spoiled ballot papers, giving Angie a two vote lead. Electoral Commission adjudicators were called to examine the result and ordered a second recount, completed by the following morning, confirming Angie as Town Councillor by the slimmest of margins. Beatrice was livid and Angie ecstatic, unaware that the euphoria would last as long as a honeymoon.

Chapter 3 – Summer to Autumn

July

Carter's flight had been long and uneventful and he'd enjoyed his layover in London, only his second visit to the City. Catching up on his sleep had been secondary and he'd wanted to see more of the sights that England's Capital had to offer. His last leg was a morning flight to Leeds-Bradford airport and the pilot had switched on the 'fasten seat belts' sign, ready for landing. The cloud was low, so his view of Yorkshire would have to wait until their descent. He heard the flaps being deployed and the clunk, clunk as the wheels engaged, ready for the landing. Still there was no sight of the ground. He glanced around. The cabin crew were strapped in, ready for the touch-down, no sign of any issues, smiling, chatting to each other. Flying in Australia had its challenges but it looked to Carter like they were travelling blind, in thick fog. Within moments, the view cleared, a few hundred feet above the ground, the sky menacing and rain streaking horizontally across the window. The pilot placed the wheels smoothly on the tarmac of the runway, applied the brakes and the 'plane slowed, afterwards turning onto a short taxiway before parking, waiting for the ramp to be attached to the side.

"Welcome to Yorkshire," said the steward.

Carter peered out of the window, watching rain splashing, forming puddles on the ground. He unfolded his Armani jacket from where it had been resting on his knee, clumsily placing

Chapter 3 – Summer to Autumn

his arms in the sleeves in the confined space until he was 'properly suited', ready for whatever Yorkshire had to offer.

~

Dolly was expecting her guest, hearing him first as the red Audi pulled up outside of her house. She opened the door as Carter walked towards the gate, opened it and headed for her, his face beaming. Dolly stared at the young man, in his mid-to-late twenties, she would guess, with the clichéd tall, dark and handsome look. Only, he was more than good-looking, he was suave, with presence. His hand was outstretched, ready for a traditional hand-shake but Dolly had different ideas. "Welcome to Heythwaite, come in out of the rain, dear," she said, giving Carter a hug, forcing him to bend at the knees.

Dolly showed Carter through to the conservatory. Soon, he was enjoying a hot, black coffee and a bacon bap, though he hadn't been sure what was being offered when Dolly suggested it. "You won't know whether you're coming or going at the moment," said Dolly.

"The time difference, you mean? I'm okay, had a layover in London. I saw some of the sights, it's a lively city."

"That it is, dear. You probably haven't had time to do it justice and you're here for a couple of days is that right?"

"Yes, staying at the Old Oak. I've not checked in yet, they said anytime after eleven."

"You could have stayed here, dear, I've plenty of room."

Chapter 3 – Summer to Autumn

Carter smiled, his glistening white teeth framing his perfect mouth, the dark stubble enhancing his looks, as he peered at Dolly with large brown eyes.

"No need to answer, love. You need your own space, is that how you say it?"

"I guess," said Carter as he changed the subject, glancing at the key fob on the table, "Is that what I've travelled half way round the world to fetch?"

He picked it up, examined it and placed it back on the table.

"Why is it so important?"

"Search me. The boss told me to collect it and you don't argue with Jimmy."

Perceptive, Dolly glanced at Carter. Was he hiding anything? She knew that he'd be loyal to Jimmy, he was his personal assistant, after all. Deciding to abandon her interrogation, she turned to small talk, trying to discover something about the young man's life, but unearthing little. When it was time for Carter to leave, he pocketed the fob, stood and wrapped his arms warmly around Dolly. "See you around?" he said, grinning as he turned, walking out of the door to the car.

~

"An Australian, our Dora told me, staying at the Old Oak, by all accounts," said Harold.

The jungle drums of Heythwaite had been beating out their message at the arrival of a young Australian and his morning visit to Dolly, before checking-in at the pub. He'd been seen in the High Street stores, shopkeepers vying to tell him of the best

Chapter 3 – Summer to Autumn

attractions of Yorkshire. It wasn't the weather for sight-seeing, the cloud being low, though the rain had stopped, but Carter was determined to capitalise on the time available. He had two whole days before he had to make the return flight, something he placed at the back of his mind, for the moment. As Carter returned to the car, a van pulled in front of him, outside the sandwich shop. Daniel jumped out, glancing briefly at the newcomer, realising that they'd blocked his exit. "Just be a minute, grabbing a buttie. It's ordered, won't be long, promise."

"Buttie, what's a buttie," said Carter, his accent obvious.

"You're that Australian everyone's talking about," said Daniel.

"Are they?" said Carter, astonished, "I've only been here a few hours."

"That's Heythwaite, your business is everyone's business. I'm Daniel by the way." They shook hands and Carter introduced himself. He'd changed into casual clothes, Hugo Boss jeans, shirt and sweater and a pair of Adidas trainers, top of the range, looking like a male model. Daniel disappeared into the deli, returning moments later as Carter was clicking his seatbelt into place. Daniel waved, jumped into the van, the tyres screeched and they sped down the high street.

~

Angie walked into the Sandpiper's pub and looked around, seeing Daniel, she waved and made a sign, asking if he wanted a drink. He continued with the non-verbal communication,

Chapter 3 – Summer to Autumn

indicating that he'd already bought her one, by pointing to it on the table. She smiled and sauntered over to him, planting a kiss on his lips, glancing at the bronzed guy in expensive clothes seated next to Daniel. "Who's your mate?" Angie said, but she had her suspicions.

"Carter," said Carter, stretching out his hand.

Angie shook the offered palm, plonked herself beside Daniel and said, "You're the Australian."

"Does everyone know about me?"

They talked of Carter's first visit to Yorkshire and he seemed to have packed a lot into the day: dales, moors, castles, small towns and villages. He was intending to go to York the following day and then onto the coast. He wanted to walk a little of the Cleveland Way whilst he was in England and had been told that the stretch near Whitby was worth seeing. Angie quizzed Carter about Australia and they spoke of his visits to New Zealand too. Daniel watched as Angie asked the questions. She was intense, interested in what Carter was saying. The evening swept by, with Daniel and Angie enjoying Carter's company. Carter was starting to flag, deciding to turn in as it was eleven o'clock, his last few days a whirlwind of activity. After Carter left, Angie turned to Daniel and looked into his eyes, a grin decorating her face, "Bit fit, isn't he?"

Daniel smiled back and replied, "Too perfect, bet he's gay."

"You wish, Daniel Taylor," said Angie.

~

Chapter 3 – Summer to Autumn

It was seven thirty in the morning and Angie was at the bus stop waiting for her journey to Skipton station and then on to Leeds. A red Audi pulled up beside her and the window wound down. A smiling Carter shouted across to her, asking her where she was heading.

"Leeds. You're up early. If you're going to the coast, it's the wrong direction, but you can take me to the station if you like. It doesn't take you far out of your way."

Carter cleared the map from the passenger seat and Angie jumped in as Carter paused the satellite navigator. "You'll have to give me directions," he said, accelerating away.

"Down to the end, then left, follow the signs to Skipton, it's only a few miles. Where you heading for today, Carter?"

"York, then I want to see Flamborough head and then go north, up the coast. My grandpa used to tell me about this part of the world, he's not around now. He mentioned puffins, guillemots and razorbills at Bempton Cliffs. He spoke fondly of Whitby and there were a couple of smaller places, Robin Hood's Bay and Staithes. I've seen photos of grandpa walking the Cleveland Way and it goes through both of them. I'm going to retrace a few of his steps. If I had longer, I'd do the trek."

"It's tough in places, especially the Hambleton and Cleveland hills. Can't you stay longer? Seems a long way for a couple of days."

"No, not this time. Jimmy, my boss, wants me back by the weekend. He's paid a lot for this trip." Carter changed the subject and they spoke of life in Heythwaite, Angie's job and

Chapter 3 – Summer to Autumn

about Perth. Too soon, Carter pulled up at Skipton railway station and Angie opened the door, turning towards Carter as she did, gazing into his chocolate coloured eyes. "Thanks for the lift. Safe journey."

"Enjoy your day," said Carter in return, his stare tunnelling into hers, unsettling her.

She stood at the entrance to the station and watched as he drove out onto the main road. 'Maybe it's as well you're leaving," she whispered to herself.

~

Angie's first Town Council meeting was the same evening as Carter's last day in Yorkshire. During her election campaign she'd advertised herself as the 'listening voice of Heythwaite'. Naïve of the council's procedures, she was overwhelmed by their weight. It became apparent quickly that the bureaucracy existed to maintain the status quo or prevent initiatives from being tabled. One of the primary tasks of the new council was to elect a chair and the railroading commenced immediately when the existing chair, Councillor Amanda Braithwaite, was proposed for the post and seconded. Angie had little time to catch her breath before Ms Braithwaite was duly elected as leader. As motion after tedious motion was discussed, she came to realise how little power a Town Councillor had. Worse, her youth, in this temple of the aged, meant that she was ignored or patronised. It annoyed her but she held her temper in check, watching Amanda working her magic, Angie deciding to bide her time: listen and learn. This woman was a master of manipulation and there was much that she could teach Angie. It

Chapter 3 – Summer to Autumn

was late when the council meeting finished. She'd arranged to meet Daniel in the pub at nine o'clock, but it was now ten. She popped her head around the bar door, spotting her boyfriend in the corner, chatting to a friend. She waved and he stood, making his way over to her.

"Took longer than you thought?" he asked.

"It was tedious, Dan."

"You still got time for a drink?"

Angie affirmed strongly and, within minutes, they were seated in the corner with their ales, Angie telling Daniel about the Town Council meeting. He listened patiently, wondering whether he should have encouraged her to stand for election. Daniel knew that these were early days, confident that Angie would learn quickly and stamp her personality on the affairs of the council. Angie asked whether Daniel had seen Carter as she'd been hoping to catch him before his departure. Daniel told her that he'd left already, staying at Leeds-Bradford airport, as he had an early flight to London the following morning and then a connection to Perth, via Dubai. The look of disappointment in her eyes was tangible and it disturbed Daniel. "He popped in here, before he left. He gave you a lift this morning, he told me."

"Yes, saw me at the bus stop and dropped me in Skipton. Did he enjoy his day?" said Angie.

"Running around like a mad man. York, Scarborough, Filey, Flamborough, Robin Hood's Bay, Whitby, Staithes and Saltburn. A real whistle stop tour."

Chapter 3 – Summer to Autumn

"He made it then! I doubted that he'd do it all. His grandad lived around here and Carter wanted to walk a little in his shoes. Looks like he succeeded. I wonder if he'll be back?"

Daniel glanced at Angie. She'd been different since Carter's arrival and he'd felt her pulling away, imperceptibly at first, but it was accelerating. Now Carter had gone, perhaps they could return to normal? Daniel hoped so. Carter had left a couple of his business cards with Daniel, one for each of them. Daniel would keep them to himself.

~

It was Friday, the day before the prestigious annual Allotment Growers Championship and the three septuagenarians were examining their crops, deciding which specimens to select for the competition. Harold had painted marker sticks red, blue and yellow; red was for their first choices, blue for second and yellow for third. On Harold's left side was Walter, with Bert on his right, as they walked at the edge of the plot. They discussed each row of vegetables in turn and Harold placed a coloured sign against a plant, as they agreed their classifications. After completion, it was time to pick their competition produce, take them home and prepare them for the championship, an elaborate undertaking. The vegetables had to be clean, with leafy vegetables soaked or sprayed with water and stored in a cool place until judging. Vegetables bearing fruit, like tomatoes or cucumbers needed rubbing with a wet cloth, then stored in a dry place. Root crops had to be soaked soon after harvest, then soil removed, usually under running water. A cardinal sin was to scrub or brush vegetables. Presentation mattered too, with

Chapter 3 – Summer to Autumn

their entries arranged artistically on white card, labelled with the variety of produce. In this annual competition, showmanship mattered as much as quality and the three amigos were adept at it. They were confident that they would clean up the prizes this year. On allotment thirty, Beatrice and Ambrose were selecting their competition specimens, Beatrice carrying a shallow basket to collect the produce that she chose, Ambrose performing the harvesting. She'd restricted her entries at the prior year's competition but, this year, she had fruit or vegetable for each category, plus an entry for jams, aiming to usurp Dora's prize. She too was positive about her chances of winning, her goal, a win in every category.

~

At nine o'clock the community hall opened and competitors were allowed into the hall to setup their exhibits. Judging was at ten thirty and the exhibits would be open to the public at noon, with prize-giving at three thirty. Dora and Harold brushed by Beatrice and Ambrose, Harold making for his competition space and Dora storming over to the table, now filling with jams and then on to the cake stall. Officials took entry forms from competitors, providing labels with numbers in return, to be associated with entries so that they would remain anonymous for judging. Bert and Walter entered the hall together, Bert nodded an acknowledgement to Ambrose before he and Walter joined Harold. They spent the next hour arranging their produce under the occasional eye of Dora, joined by Elsie, Bert's wife. Sharply, at ten thirty, all of the competitors were expelled from the hall and the judges took

Chapter 3 – Summer to Autumn

their place. As was the practice for the Allotment Growers Competition, the Old Oak opened it's doors early so Walter, Harold and Bert trooped over, Walter ordering two pints of Theakston's best bitter and a Black Sheep beer for himself. They seated themselves at their usual table, eyeing up their allotment pals, also competition, who'd had the same idea. The banter was good natured, each knowing that the hard work had been done, nothing else left to do but await the verdict of the adjudicators.

~

At noon, a crowd of allotment holders huddled around the blackboard that contained the results of the Allotment Holders Competition for this year. They were deathly silent.

Vegetable Classes

Class 1: Courgettes, *Winner Victorious 30*

Class 2: Carrots, Single Variety, *Winner Victorious 30*

Class 3: Beetroot, *Winner Victorious 30*

Class 4: Broad Bean Pods, *Winner Victorious 30*

Class 5: Potatoes, Single Variety, *Winner Victorious 30*

Class 6: Onions, Single Variety, *Winner Victorious 30*

Class 7: Pea Pods, *Winner Victorious 30*

Class 8: Cabbage on a one inch stalk, *Winner Victorious 30*

Class 9: Rhubarb Sticks, *Winner Victorious 30*

Class 10: Lettuce, *Winner Victorious 30*

Class 11: Spring Onions, *Winner Victorious 30*

Chapter 3 – Summer to Autumn

Class 12: 8 Strawberries, *Winner Victorious 30*

Class 13: 8 Raspberries, *Winner Victorious 30*

Class 14: Tomatoes with stalks, *Winner Victorious 30*

Bert took off his cap and rubbed his head, shocked at what he was reading, barely believing his eyes. "She's won 'em all," said Harold, as he turned to the 'Jams and Conserves' list.

"We'll be a laughing stock," said Walter.

"Dora's done a clean sweep with the jams. She's first in every category."

"Watch out," said Bert, glancing towards the centre of the hall, "She's heading over here, and she doesn't look too pleased."

"Well," Dora said, stopping, framed by the doorway, hands on hips, spittle forming droplets in the air as she spoke, "Not a single win. Call yourself gardeners. You're losing your touch lads. I'm beginning to wonder what you do over at that plot."

"We had second prizes," said Walter, weakly, but Dora didn't stay to hear his repost, trudging out of the village hall door, leaving a draught of air behind her.

"I don't envy you tonight," said Walter, smiling.

~

"It was pretty decisive," said Dolly, "Beatrice took all of the prizes in the fruit and vegetable categories." It was another Wednesday with Betsy and Dolly waiting for the morning bus to Skipton for the market. They'd been discussing the Allotment Growers Competition and the unequivocal success

Chapter 3 – Summer to Autumn

of Beatrice and Ambrose. "People are saying that she didn't stick to all of the rules," said Betsy.

"Sour grapes, I should think."

"Her displays were on white card, like they should be, but she'd had them printed, showing the vegetable variety on display, and they were edged in gold," said Betsy, "It was obvious to the judges who's entries they were."

"The boys seem to be resigned to their defeat. They were disappointed at first but they've moved on," said Dolly.

"Which is more than can be said for Dora," said Betsy.

"Yes, she bent my ear about it the other day. Once she has her teeth into something, she won't let go." Dolly was pleased to see the bus turn the corner and it gave her a chance to change the subject. Hamid, the bus driver, pulled up to the stop, opening the doors to allow a young couple off the bus.

"Morning Missus," Hamid said as Betsy stepped forward.

Betsy placed her pass on the receptacle until she heard a 'beep' sound and then said to the driver, "How's that little boy of yours?"

"Eating me out of house and home, never stops," said Hamid.

Dolly stepped forward and put her card in place until she heard the sound and then added, "And the baby girl, Hamid? She must be sitting up by now."

"She's crawling around Mrs Jackson, such a happy little'n, always laughing."

Chapter 3 – Summer to Autumn

Dolly smiled at the driver then moved slowly down the bus, Betsy rushing to grab their usual seat. Hamid watched in his mirror, making sure that the ladies were seated before setting off. As they pulled away, before the bus turned towards the bridge at the foot of the hill, Dolly leaned towards Betsy and said, in a hushed voice, "I spoke to Andrew yesterday."

Betsy turned her head towards, Dolly, loosening her headscarf to make herself comfortable, but said nothing. "Jimmy told Carter to give the key to Andrew, for safe keeping. I think that he and Carter have been talking."

"Bonny lad, that one. I bet he turned a few heads when he was here," said Betsy, grinning.

"Angie's by all accounts, according to Bert," said Dolly.

"I thought she was with Daniel," said Betsy.

"She is, but let's get back to Andrew," said Dolly, in a low voice, "I think the lad's convinced Jimmy that he should confide in his solicitor. Andrew's not saying, of course, but I think he knows what's in the safe."

"What makes you think that?"

"Just something Andrew mentioned. He never could hide anything from me."

"So, what's in the box?"

"Oh, I don't know that, dear. He wouldn't betray a confidence."

"Then we're no further forward?" said Betsy.

Chapter 3 – Summer to Autumn

"A little," said Dolly, smiling, "I know who was responsible for the break-ins."

Betsy gasped as she said, "You do?"

"It was the way that Andrew told me that raised my suspicions. When I asked him point-blank, he couldn't deny it."

"Who did then?"

"Jimmy, though I don't think he meant for them to happen. He wanted the key-fob back pretty badly. He paid some private detectives to follow the trail."

"And they were over enthusiastic!" said Betsy.

"Exactly, crossed a line, was how Andrew justified it. I told him that it caused much distress in Heythwaite. You know, Jimmy told me that he was sorry, you remember, when he left the wedding party?"

"Yes, I do recall, you looked preoccupied," said Betsy.

"It does explain why he was so odd, probably remorseful."

"I wonder if we'll ever find out what this was really about?" said Betsy.

"Probably not in our lifetime."

August

"Elsie and Dora have been talking," said Harold. Bert knew what was coming so he waited for Harold to continue. "They're putting in a complaint to the committee."

Chapter 3 – Summer to Autumn

"I know, about the display cards," said Bert, "I think they should let it rest."

Dora was sure that the judges were biased in favour of Beatrice. She'd said 'that woman' had used an unfair advantage and the distinctive printing and edging had identified the crops as theirs. The rules had been broken, the results void, it was as clear as that, and a fully loaded locomotive would not stop Dora. "What does Elsie think?" said Harold.

"Oh, you know," said Bert, uncommitted.

"Oh, I do," said Harold, smiling.

"What're you two gossiping about?" said Walter, his basket full of produce he'd been collecting from the plot, "As if I didn't know. The complaint I would think."

"Aye, that's right," said Bert.

"Let them do what they want," said Walter, glancing at his crop, "This is what it's really about, the harvest. Nothing quite like fresh vegetables, straight from the ground, into the pot."

Harold examined the colourful array of produce on display and asked Walter what he was making, knowing that there would be plenty left over to share. Walter's recipes were tasty, full of Caribbean spices and chillies, different to the fare that Dora dished up. Walter told Bert and Harold that he was preparing a black eyed pea stew, with cobblers, a north country twist on his mother's recipe. "They'd call it 'fusion food' in one of those fancy restaurants," said Walter, laughing.

"And charge an arm and a leg for it too," said Bert.

"You're making my mouth water," said Harold.

Chapter 3 – Summer to Autumn

"There'll be plenty left. Are you coming over to the allotment tomorrow?"

"I am now, especially as I know you've got grub."

~

Councillor Amanda Braithwaite chaired the Allotment Growers Association committee meeting on the first Thursday of the month so that it didn't clash with her town council responsibilities. It was a small and friendly group of the elderly, more a horticulturalists outing than a formal meeting. Annie Taylor, a short plump lady with wiry grey hair, outspoken and a fussy manner, was the secretary. She was also Daniel's grandmother and had been discussing with the treasurer, David Wilson, the break-up of Daniel and Angie's relationship that had occurred that morning. David, a tall, serious man, of slim build, well into his sixties, listened politely; he hadn't been aware that Daniel and Angie had been a couple so was delighted when Amanda called the meeting to order, ending the conversation. She dispensed with formalities efficiently, listened to David's dull explanation of the organisation's finances and then moved on to committee business. "Annie, do you have a reference for the complaint we've received?" Amanda said, addressing the secretary. Annie confirmed that she'd allocated a number to the letter and gave it to Amanda who continued, "It concerns the annual competition and cites an irregularity."

Beatrice glanced around at the other committee members who were studiously avoiding eye contact. The letter hadn't been circulated to the committee, but it appeared to her, that some

Chapter 3 – Summer to Autumn

members had prior knowledge of its contents. Beatrice listened as Amanda explained the letter's grievance, that the cards had been printed professionally, pointing to the identity of the exhibit owner, removing anonymity, possibly influencing the judges. Beatrice sniffed; the communique was polished, whoever had written it received assistance, she was sure. "This concerns you, Beatrice," said Amanda, "I must ask you to leave whilst we discuss the matter."

Beatrice smiled as she rose to her feet and left the room, the silence pervading as she gently closed the door and walked to the kitchen to prepare a coffee.

~

Walter had reheated his black eyed pea stew on the small stove in their shed at the allotment, the three friends seated in a line on the bench at the edge of their plot. Each had a helping of Walter's spicy recipe plus a dumpling-like cobbler. "This is grand, lad, real tasty," said Harold.

"What are the spices?" said Bert.

"It's a Caribbean mix of allspice, nutmeg, cinnamon, plus chillies of course. It should have cloves but I think they overpower, so I don't bother."

"It goes so well with the cobbler," said Bert, lapping up the last of the juices with the dumpling.

"I'm glad you like it," said Walter, beaming.

Harold's phone rang and he glanced at the display. As it was Dora calling, his face betrayed alarm as he answered the call. The buzz of Dora's voice could be heard as Harold offered the

Chapter 3 – Summer to Autumn

odd 'yes' and 'really' but mostly Harold listened and Dora talked. Expectant stares faced Harold as he disconnected the call. It was rare for Dora to bother Harold when they were gardening. "Dora's complaint," he said, "Its been upheld."

"I'll be damned," said Bert, "Does that mean ..."

Bert didn't finish as Harold interrupted, "She's disqualified from this year's competition. We've been declared winners of all of the vegetable classes."

"That'll please Dora," said Walter.

"It has, and me," said Harold, beaming, "but there's something else, just as good."

"Don't keep us in suspense, spit it out," said Bert.

"Beatrice has resigned from the committee."

"Are you sure she wasn't pushed out?" said Walter.

~

Beatrice was fussing with a vase of flowers, arranging and then rearranging them. Ambrose knew better than to interfere; it was Beatrice's way of coping with disappointments. Their bed linen had been changed, house was spotless, windows cleaned, inside and out and the garden was next on her list. She wore headphones to keep the world out and listened to podcasts of plays from BBC radio. Beatrice's anger simmered just below the surface but she kept it in check. Ambrose and Beatrice had been through much and he knew that his wife would need to cope in her own way. He gave her the space and support she needed. They'd been through worse; in the grand scheme, this problem was piffling. Early in their marriage Beatrice

Chapter 3 – Summer to Autumn

miscarried mid term. When they tried again, the same happened, later in the pregnancy, causing a medical emergency. Beatrice was close to death, frail, slipping away, and that image still haunted Ambrose, decades later. The doctor had told them that the risk to Beatrice from another pregnancy was severe and they decided to forgo a family. Beatrice had kept herself active since that time, her coping strategy, but Ambrose knew that her pain, hidden to most, was acute. 'She'll bounce back', he thought and he was certain that she would.

~

"Hello, dear," said Dolly, spotting Angie waiting at the bus stop for her morning journey to Skipton railway station.

"Hi, Dolly. You're looking nice. You off somewhere?"

"Just a bit of shopping, then I'm meeting Betsy at Edwina's. You must be off to work are you? You're a bit late."

"I've been in the library, finishing a design. We're on site for the next few days so I'll be away."

"How's Daniel?"

"Oh, haven't you heard? We've split up, Dan and me."

"No, dear, I hadn't, but that's your business, not mine," Dolly said, smiling. Dolly had been surprised at the news but hid it from Angie. She'd thought that they made a good couple but she'd seen much in her long life; little surprised her. Angie and Daniel were young, plenty of time for them to meet the right partners, if they wanted. Relationships were different to when she was their age but, looking back, she wouldn't have spent her time differently. After saying goodbye to Angie, Dolly

Chapter 3 – Summer to Autumn

meandered up the hill, chatting to those she met along the way, popping into shops for the few items she wished to buy and then making her way to the coffee shop where she found Betsy already seated. The proprietor, Edwina, waited until Dolly arrived before greeting her regular customers and taking their order, one that rarely varied. From Lancashire, she'd resisted stocking cherry bakewell but had relented since her friendship with the ladies had grown, though she preferred the 'real bakewell tarts' herself. As she delivered the order to the table, Dolly turned to Edwina, saying, "Did you know that Angie and Daniel aren't going out together?"

"Yes, Dolly. Bert told me. Daniel's not taking it well, apparently. It was Angie who terminated their relationship."

"That's a pity. I thought they made a lovely couple but there's nowt so queer as folk, as they say."

"That they do Dolly, that they do," said Edwina, walking away.

Dolly turned to Betsy and they talked about Dolly's shopping before discussing Beatrice and the events at the Allotment Growers Association committee meeting. Their views were aligned and both knew where to lay the blame, at Dora's door.

"It seems to me, that Beatrice's produce was the best, so should have won," said Betsy, "I don't think the printed card would have swayed anyone, not in Yorkshire."

"No, dear, probably the opposite," said Dolly, "You know how we don't like showy folk around here."

Chapter 3 – Summer to Autumn

"Dora's had it in for her since Beatrice arrived. It's the same thing, Dolly, too flamboyant for Dora's liking," said Betsy.

"You know, Betsy, I might just pop round later and see how Beatrice is doing. She's probably upset, what with the Town Council elections and now this. A woman can take only so much."

~

It was unseasonably cold in Perth, Western Australia, at ten degrees Celsius, forcing Jimmy to wear an overcoat. He and Carter were walking in the light rain as they returned from a customer meeting. In the blustery wind there was little conversation and they strode earnestly to reach Jimmy's building. Inside, they walked up a flight of stairs, into the office and removed their coats. They'd met an important client and Carter led on the negotiations, having done the homework. The initial relationship had been with Jimmy but Carter was respected by the customer and could have sealed the deal himself. Jimmy knew it and so did Carter. His recent trip to Sydney, in consort with Jimmy's son, Ryan, who ran the eastern operation, the most profitable arm, had been successful. Ryan valued Carter and wanted him in Sydney, as a full partner. He'd been forthright with his father, telling him that he'd lose Carter unless he offered him something tangible, a substantial role, with shares to lock him into the company.

"Do you want a coffee, Jimmy?" said Carter.

"In a moment, perhaps, rest your legs, lad."

Chapter 3 – Summer to Autumn

Carter glanced at his boss wondering what was coming as he took a seat opposite Jimmy. "You seem a bit unsettled," said Jimmy, intending to continue, but Carter cut in.

"A few things happening at home, Sophie and I have split."

Carter rarely discussed his personal life, so Jimmy was surprised as he said, "I'm sorry, I didn't know."

"It won't affect my work," said Carter, staring into Jimmy's wizened eyes.

"It hasn't, as I said, I didn't know."

"Is there a problem?" said Carter, putting Jimmy on the back foot. This wasn't going well.

"Not at all. Look, let's start again, I'll not pry into your personal life."

Jimmy cut to the chase, telling Carter about his conversation with Ryan and offering him a bigger role in the company, split between Sydney and Perth initially and then moving to Sydney. Carter listened, then enquired about the future of the operation in Perth. Though smaller than the eastern element, it was still a substantial part of Jimmy's empire. "The seat of power is in Sydney, lad. You need to be where the decisions are made. Once you're settled in, Ryan wants you to recruit someone to run the operation here. I'm finally going to retire."

"Can't see you doing that, Jimmy," said Carter.

"You tell that to Babs."

"You want to think about it?" said Jimmy.

Chapter 3 – Summer to Autumn

"It's a great opportunity, thanks. I'd like to talk to Ryan, if that's okay?"

"Sure, now, how about that coffee?"

"One more thing, Jimmy."

Jimmy looked up at Carter, who smiled.

"I'd like a couple of weeks holiday, next week?"

"That sudden, where you off to?"

"Heythwaite, unfinished business," said Carter.

~

The look of surprise on Beatrice's face when she opened the door to Dolly was difficult for her to disguise. Dolly looked small, standing in the porch of the substantial house amongst the flowering plants and ornamental shrubs in pots and tubs. They exchanged greetings and Beatrice invited Dolly in to her stylish kitchen, resplendent with its granite work surfaces, fitted cupboards and modern appliances.

"It's nice to see you Dolly, what brings you out this way?"

"I wanted to see how you were, after the allotment shenanigans."

"That's nice of you. I've had a few days of cleaning, you know," said Beatrice, glancing at her guest, smiling.

"That works for me too, dear. Takes my mind off things."

"Next to the many things happening in the world, it's a small thing, but it stung a little, I confess. A coffee, or tea?"

"Coffee would be lovely," said Dolly, as Beatrice offered her a seat at the peninsular unit at the centre of the grand kitchen.

Chapter 3 – Summer to Autumn

Conversation flowed, as did a couple of hours when Dolly glanced at the clock. She had a hair appointment and needed to leave. Beatrice offered to drop her at the hairdresser but Dolly wouldn't hear of it. She had enough time and the walk would be beneficial. As Beatrice stood on the doorstep, waving goodbye to her surprise visitor, she told Dolly that they should meet again, and she meant every word.

~

Angie walked up Heythwaite's High Street, a broad grin decorating her face. She'd taken her second practical driving test and had passed, after failing the first time. She'd been annoyed with herself, more accustomed to succeeding, so had taken an intensive two day driving course, at considerable cost, now worth every penny. "You look like the cat that got the cream," said Betsy as she turned the corner and spotted Angie.

"Oh, hello Mrs Longbottom. Is it that obvious? I've just passed my driving test."

"Well done, lass. First time wasn't it?"

"Second."

"Well, you've done it, that's what matters. I haven't driven for years," said Betsy.

Angie was surprised for she'd never seen Betsy behind the wheel of a car. Betsy explained that she'd had a minor accident, when she was in her fifties, and it had damaged her confidence. She'd stopped driving and Dick, the garage owner, had purchased the car from her. "Wouldn't want to drive now,

Chapter 3 – Summer to Autumn

and the buses are fine," said Betsy, "It'll make a difference to you, mark my words, lass."

Angie smiled and was about to walk on when Betsy said, as a passing remark, "I hear that you and young Daniel have broken-up. He's quite cut up, Bert tells me."

"Is he?" said Angie, fazed by Betsy's remark, "I didn't know, haven't seen around him much."

"Annie, his grandma, you know her?" said Betsy as Angie nodded, "She told me he's moping around, under everyone's feet."

"I'm sorry to hear that," said Angie, uncomfortable, "Look, I'm late, I need to dash. It was nice talking to you." Rushing down the street, Angie's elated feeling was receding as guilt took its place.

~

"You're doing what? When?" said Angie, glancing at the small screen of her phone and the bronzed face decorating it. The call from Australia had become a regular daily occurrence. They started after Angie had contacted Carter using a smartphone app's messaging service when she'd discovered that Daniel hadn't passed on Carter's business card. She'd been livid with him and it had eroded trust between them. Carter had tagged Angie in a Facebook post, later resulting in an exchange of contact details and the revelation about Daniel's conduct. Across the miles, an impractical, unlikely relationship was blossoming, something neither had expected, nor wanted. Nevertheless, the alchemy of Eros bubbled, his arrows

Chapter 3 – Summer to Autumn

spanning the impossible distance. "Next week, for two weeks," said Carter's voice, made tinny-sounding by the phone speaker.

Angie was stunned and silent.

"Say something, even if it's that you don't want me to come."

"Of course I do," said Angie, her eyes wide, "I'm a bit shocked, that's all."

"Am I moving too quickly for you?"

"Probably, but what the heck," said Angie.

"So, you're pleased I'm coming?"

"You bet," said Angie.

~

Dolly was still shaking as she seated herself away from the window in Edwina's Coffee House, a steaming cup of sweet tea in front of her and Edwina fussing around her. Tears streamed down Dolly's face and she wiped them away with a lace edged handkerchief that she'd taken from her bag. Dolly had been walking down the high street when she heard the roaring and screeching of brakes from an articulated lorry thundering down the hill. She'd turned to see the truck mount the pavement, hit the bus shelter and then veer back onto the road, overturning as it did, spilling its load onto the highway. Other cars acted swiftly, veering out of the way or halting away from the commotion. One car was not so lucky and Dick, the garage owner, was driving it, testing its operation after a repair. He was caught between the runaway truck and a van, the cab of the lorry landing squarely on Dick's vehicle. A young man called the emergency services and Dolly watched as they

Chapter 3 – Summer to Autumn

sprang into action. First, the fire brigade arrived and shortly afterwards an ambulance and the police, who took control of the situation. Several burly firemen, using heavy machinery, cut open Dick's car and gingerly extracted him from the wreckage, leading him to the awaiting medical team who strapped Dick to a stretcher, placed an oxygen mask over his face and started to look for his vital signs. Dolly watched, dumbstruck, hand over her mouth, as Dick was loaded into the ambulance, his face silver grey. The doors slammed shut, sirens blared for a moment and a policeman cleared the way for the paramedics as they sped away to Airedale's accident and emergency hospital. A tear formed in the corner of Dolly's eye as she revisited her last view of Dick in her mind. In a daze, Dolly barely remembered Edwina guiding her towards the café, weakly regaining her faculties only when she picked up a cup of tea, England's answer to every crisis. "It's sweet tea, love. You've had a shock, sip it slowly," said Edwina.

"Thank you, dear," said Dolly, gazing towards her host, "How much do I owe you?"

"Oh, don't worry about that. Just breathe slowly, you are shaking, look at you."

Dolly drank the tea and Edwina replaced it with another, listening to Dolly as she relived the events of the last half hour. Outside, the clean-up crew had arrived and a large crane was being used to right the articulated lorry. The driver was being quizzed by a young policeman, supported by a woman officer. By the time that Dolly had completed her second cup of tea, traffic was moving again and Dolly turned to the subject of

Chapter 3 – Summer to Autumn

Dick. "He looked pallid, Edwina. I hope he's going to be alright. There was blood on his leg."

"I wonder if Madge knows?"

"Oh, dear, I'd not thought of Madge. She would want to be with him."

Edwina offered to call the hairdresser and, picking up her mobile phone, dialled her number. Another stylist answered and, when Edwina asked to speak to Madge, the colleague told her that Madge had gone to Airedale Hospital, explaining about Dick's accident. Dolly watched, but heard only Edwina's side of the conversation. "She's with him," said Edwina as she disconnected the call.

"Thank the Lord," said Dolly.

"All we can do now is wait," said Edwina.

~

Alex and Iggy, the Polish builders, were working in a shop opposite the bus shelter when they heard the commotion. They rushed outside, witnessing the devastation materialising before them. The bus shelter was demolished by the truck, toughened glass shattering into thousands of pieces, steel frame folding like origami. They saw the driver struggling to retain control as he pulled on the wheel, trying to coax the vehicle back onto the road. It was fortunate that a bus had left recently, the bus stop empty, otherwise the consequences would have been dire. The camber of the pavement edge caught the truck driver off-guard and the lorry leaned beyond its centre of gravity. Alex watched in disbelief as the vehicle, in apparent slow motion, started to

Chapter 3 – Summer to Autumn

topple, smoke escaping from the tyres, brakes screeching and an acrid smell in the air. Iggy pulled Alex into the shop, fearing that the lorry was heading for them. As he did, cars scattered, or stopped as they saw the events unfolding before them, except for one car, trapped between the truck and a van. With the truck stationary, on its side, Alex and Iggy rushed forward to see if they could assist. Soon, they were ushered away as the police took control and the other emergency services stepped into the fray, their efficiency and competence on display for all to testify. The builders returned to their work, Alex brewing a pot of strong coffee to ward off the shock. Gareth, an optician, was starting a practice in Heythwaite. He'd worked for a prestigious practice in Leeds but wanted to branch out on his own, close to Skipton, but a rural practice. Heythwaite was fortunate that he'd chosen their location, for he was skilled and his knowledge current. Gareth had done his homework; the town had a high proportion of middle-aged, elderly and wealthy people, his ideal clients. He'd asked around for recommendations for workmen and Edwina had suggested Alex and Iggy for she was content with the jobs they'd done for her. That's how the Polish builders happened to be in Heythwaite on that fateful day. Gareth arrived as the ambulance took Dick away. He was on foot, unable to gain access to the High Street, parking outside of the town. He wanted to open the practice in two weeks as he'd left his previous job and money was leaching away on the new venture. After asking about the incident, Gareth examined the progress Alex and Iggy had made and was delighted. Partitions had been built to separate his consulting room from the fitting

Chapter 3 – Summer to Autumn

and reception areas. The reception desk, shelving and spectacle display cabinets were in progress. Gareth was confident that, by the end of the week, painting and final touches would be all that were left to accomplish. His expensive equipment could be delivered and he could distribute the leaflets he'd had produced to houses around Heythwaite.

~

Betsy was cleaning the table in Dolly's kitchen when the door bell rang melodiously, like the chimes of an ancient clock. She'd done some shopping for Dolly, who hadn't ventured out since the incident. Dick's condition had been serious and he'd needed an operation on his left leg, pinning his bones together as they'd broken in several places. He'd been under intensive care for the first day but had been transferred to a general ward after the surgical intervention. His condition was improving but Dick was unlikely to be home for a week, at best. Dolly walked down the hall to the front door, opened it and struggled to keep her mouth clamped shut at the sight before her. "How are you, Dolly?" said Beatrice, holding out a bunch of colourful dahlias from her garden.

"Are they for me?" said Dolly, regaining her composure.

"They are. I'd heard about the lorry in the High Street. I wanted to see if you were alright."

"I'm forgetting my manners," said Dolly, "Do come in. I was just going to make a cup of tea." Dolly showed Beatrice through to the conservatory and Betsy saw her before Beatrice saw Betsy.

Chapter 3 – Summer to Autumn

"Good morning to you," said Betsy.

"I don't think we've met formally, but I have seen you about town. Betsy isn't it?" said Beatrice, knowing fine well who was before her.

"Everyone knows Betsy," said Dolly, intervening before Betsy had a chance to speak. Betsy made a cup of tea as Dolly joined Beatrice in the conservatory overlooking the small garden, now decorated with late summer blooms, cosmos dominating. They talked of the runaway truck and Dick's condition, Dolly re-telling the event, it becoming easier each time. She'd been reluctant to venture into the High Street again, despite Betsy telling her that the only remnant from the incident was the lack of a bus shelter. The council had taken away the remains of the old one, a new one apparently on order. Beatrice listened sympathetically and confirmed what Betsy had told Dolly. Betsy arrived with tea and biscuits, in china cups, resplendent with matching saucers and on a wooden tray. Dolly smiled at Betsy who winked at her, the meaning obvious to them both. Dolly poured the tea and offered Beatrice a biscuit, which she took, pushing her backside into the chair as she sipped the hot drink. "I told Dolly, she needs to get back up the High Street, face her devils," said Betsy.

"I wouldn't quite have put it that way, but Betsy is right, Dolly," said Beatrice.

Dolly nodded, glancing at Betsy, a grin sweeping across her face. "I wondered if I could put something by you, test the water, as it were," said Beatrice.

Chapter 3 – Summer to Autumn

"What's that," said Betsy.

Beatrice smiled as she said, "That unfortunate incident, bad though it was, could have been much worse."

"Yes, dear, if the bus had been late, well I dread to think. There were ten people waiting at that stop just a few minutes earlier,"

"That's my point. The council has talked of a bypass for the town for how long?" said Beatrice.

"Forty years that I now of," said Betsy.

"Oh, at least, dear," said Dolly.

"Well, perhaps we should do something about it. Force their hand and start a public protest. Only by the grace of God have we not had carnage in Heythwaite," said Beatrice.

Dolly glanced at Betsy. She rarely stood up to be counted, happy to let others take the lead. This time was different after Dolly had witnessed the disaster unfolding before her. She couldn't stand by and let it happen again, not without a fight. "What are you suggesting, dear?" said Dolly.

"A campaign. Petition the County Council, mobilise the Town Council. I'm sure that young girl who was elected last time will support us, even if Amanda Braithwaite sits on the fence," said Beatrice.

"Angie, you mean. Yes, I think she will," said Dolly.

"Are you in?" said Beatrice.

"Try and stop me," said Betsy.

Chapter 3 – Summer to Autumn

"Yes, dear, I'd be delighted to join but I think you should show us how, act as the lead. I'm not very good at leading." Beatrice smiled and sipped her tea as she bit into a chocolate covered biscuit.

~

Madge stopped the van close to the gate of Dick's house and switched off the engine. They were close friends, but were not romantically attached and lived separately, both alone. Dick's home was close to his business, a garage where he and Luke, the apprentice, serviced cars. Luke had been running the operation since the accident and he broke away from his work when he heard the car turn up. He shouted a welcome to Madge, held up his dirty hands, indicating that he'd wash them and then moved to help Madge manoeuvre Dick into the house. Madge, leaving Dick in the vehicle, swung open the gate and wedged a stone against it to keep it ajar, then unlocked and opened the front door. By the time she returned to the van, Luke was at its side discussing the business with his boss. A plaster cast covered Dick's left leg, immobilising it from the knee. The seat had been pushed back to its maximum extent to accommodate his outstretched leg. "Hello Luke, how's it been today?" said Madge.

"It's been fine, nothing I can't handle," said the young man who'd risen to the occasion, handling the servicing of cars and vans during Dick's absence. Dick was pale in colour and some discomfort remained, though the severe pain was gone. Luke retrieved the crutches from the back of the van and Madge took hold of them whilst Dick swung around. Luke then helped

Chapter 3 – Summer to Autumn

Dick out of the seat, down from the vehicle, supporting him until Dick could position himself using the supports. With his apprentice's assistance, careful not to put weight on his left leg, Dick made his way along the short path to the front door, up a step and into the hall. He was pleased when he reached the lounge and could settle into his winged leather armchair. Dick's younger brother and Luke had moved a single bed downstairs into the rear lounge as it would be a few weeks before Dick could manage the steep stairs of his house. Luke took his leave, returning to his work, and Madge made a cup of tea and some lunch for her patient. She'd left the running of the hair salon to her stylists and taken a couple of weeks holiday. She'd assess the situation after that and, at present, knew where her priorities lay. Dick was home, a step on the road to recovery and she shuddered at the thought of what might have been.

~

Dolly watched as a car slid to a halt and a young woman leaned over and kissed a dark haired man. The woman opened the vehicle door, stepping out onto the path and waved as the car drifted into the road and then up the High Street. Dolly thought for a moment before the process of recognition kicked in. Angie walked towards Dolly and Dolly stopped, forcing Angie to do the same. "Good morning, Angie. Are you well?"

"I'm fine Mrs Jackson," said Angie but was interrupted by Dolly.

"Oh, call me Dolly, everyone does. Was that Carter I saw in the car? Is he over here again?"

Chapter 3 – Summer to Autumn

Angie bit her lip before she confirmed Carter's identity. What had she expected? This was Heythwaite, everyone knew everybody else's business, it went with the territory. "Good for you, dear, I hope it works out. It's a long way for a serious relationship, though," said Dolly.

"Tell me about it," said Angie her face betraying the depth of her feelings for Carter.

Dolly smiled, nodded and patted Angie's hands as she said, "You'll find a way, dear, if its meant to be. If it is, well, you grasp it while you can."

Angie gazed into Dolly's eyes, seeing the wisdom of this old lady for the first time, returning the smile as she said, "I wanted to see you anyway, Dolly."

"Yes, love."

"About the petition, how's it going by the way?"

"Most of the residents have signed it, a few we haven't managed to badger yet, but we will. It'll be ready the end of this week," said Dolly.

"That's grand," said Angie, "I've spoken to Amanda, who's basically left it to me." Dolly raised her eyes, saying nothing. She knew Amanda well as a person who liked the limelight, always in the right places, leaving the work to others, taking credit and shedding blame, a perfect politician. "Well," said Angie, continuing, "I've been in contact with the County Councillor, he's talked to Highways and, as you might guess, there isn't the budget for a bypass. I told him of the strength of feeling after the accident. How is Dick by the way?"

Chapter 3 – Summer to Autumn

"Doing well. He's looking better but his mobility is restricted, dear."

"I spoke to Luke, just after he came home. He told me that Dick looked poorly. Anyhow, the County Councillor was concerned, he's up for election again in May next year, and didn't want adverse publicity. There might be an opening there."

"That's very helpful, Angie, thank you. I'll talk to Beatrice. I think we can help the Councillor achieve that bad publicity that might just force his hand."

~

The community hall was packed, every row of chairs occupied, forcing people to stand at the rear. A cacophony of voices filled the air of the old building, its acoustics creating echoes, shadows from the past, the hall having witnessed generations of people from Heythwaite airing their causes. At the front, on the stage, was a table, behind which sat the Town Council Chair, Amanda Braithwaite, Beatrice and Dolly. To the side, on the front row of chairs was Angie with Carter seated to her left and Betsy to her right. Beatrice stood and rang a bell to command attention. Within moments the room became hushed as Beatrice explained the reason for the public meeting. She spoke passionately about the recent incident, the need for a bypass and the intransigence of the County Council. She was preaching to the converted for there was strong support for their proposition that Heythwaite needed a bypass, helped by the presence of Dick, his first outing since the accident. Beatrice went on to explain their plan. Primarily, to influence

Chapter 3 – Summer to Autumn

the Highways Department they needed money for a campaign. Persuasively, she explained where the money would be spent. They'd employ a consultant to make a firm case and a public relations organisation to influence the media. Beatrice announced that they'd need banners and placards along the High Street, finally giving an impassioned plea for volunteers for the cause. "If every family gave a hundred pounds, or even fifty, we could achieve the impossible. Tonight, I'd like you to pledge money to the campaign, we don't need money this evening, just your guarantees. There are forms at the rear of the hall, please do complete them before you leave," she said, finishing her prepared speech, and, gesturing towards Dick, she continued, "This is Dick's first outing since the terrible events that could have been so much worse. Dick, thank you for coming tonight, I know it hasn't been easy, and we're all so pleased that you are on the mend."

Beatrice lowered herself gently to her chair and Amanda took her place, asking for questions from the audience. The first question was from Dora, Harold's wife. "A hundred pounds is nowt to the likes of you, but its a lot to us pensioners."

Beatrice was about to rise to her feet when Dolly patted her on the arm and stood in her place. The hall went silent. "I'm a pensioner too, Dora. Beatrice is too modest to tell you of her contribution to the fighting fund but I can tell you it's substantial. What I witnessed that fateful day, I do not want to see again in my lifetime. We were fortunate, for there could have been untold fatalities had the truck arrived just minutes earlier. You know I'm not one to search out the limelight but I

Chapter 3 – Summer to Autumn

can't stand back and let it happen again. I ask you all to help us. We've been asking for a bypass for nigh on forty years. It's time we got off our backsides and did something."

Dolly's intervention made a difference, the remainder of the questions directed at detail, rather than the principle of the campaign. Mostly, people asked about the role of the consultants, specifically, what they would do. Beatrice explained that she'd had initial discussions with a highway specialist and she'd been told that the best way to influence the County Council was a well developed case, one with facts that they couldn't ignore. "You see," said Beatrice, "if anything happens again, God forbid, and we've produced substantial evidence to support our campaign, the County Council would be in a weak position, especially with the media. The one thing a public body fears over everything else is bad press."

As the questions petered out, the meeting closed and residents trickled towards the twin doors at the opposite end of the hall to the stage, a majority pausing to pledge money to the campaign. Just over thirty thousand pounds was promised that evening, giving their campaign wings. Additionally, twenty people came forward to volunteer to be part of the campaign team. Among them was Gareth, Heythwaite's new optician. As Carter and Angie left the hall, Angie linked her arm with Carter's and turned the corner to confront a stern faced Annie Taylor, Daniel's grandmother.

"Mrs Taylor," said Angie, "This is Carter."

"I know who you are," said Annie, turning away, marching towards the High Street.

Chapter 3 – Summer to Autumn

"What was that about?" said Carter.

"Daniel's gran," said Angie.

"Ah," said Carter, smiling, "Well, all's fair in love and war."

Angie stared at Carter, saying, "What do you mean by that?"

"It's obvious isn't it? I'm smitten, never met anyone like you. Why'd you think I travelled half way around the world? It wasn't for the weather, that's for sure, nor a strange meeting in the village hall."

Angie leaned forward, kissing Carter and, as she pulled away, said, "Carter McBride, I love you, can't believe I'm saying this. I'm smitten too and I'm scared."

"Scared, that's an odd thing to say, why?"

"Well, you're going back in a week. What do we do then?"

"Come back with me, let's get married, as soon as we can, let's not wait."

"Who'ah, what are you saying? You're serious, aren't you?"

"Deadly, Angie. I can't live without you."

Angie was silent for a moment and looked away, tears forming in her eyes. She wiped them away as Carter spoke softly, "Moving too quickly again, am I?"

"A bit, you're overwhelming, on many levels. We hardly know each other."

"You're the one, Angie, I'm sure of it."

Angie stared into Carter's eyes, framing his perfect face. How could she be this lucky? Indecision was a rare emotion of hers. In her heart, she wanted to take up Carter's offer but her head

Chapter 3 – Summer to Autumn

was hesitating, thinking the practical. The moment was now, Carter would leave in a week. Could she let him slip away? What had Dolly said? 'If its meant to be, grasp it while you can', that was it.

"I'm coming with you, back to Australia," said Angie, breathlessly, her head spinning.

Carter kneeled, looked up at Angie and said, "Angie, will you marry me?"

"Get up you plonker," said Angie, "Of course I will. Are we mad?"

"Probably, but in a good way," said Carter.

~

Angie had taken some holiday during Carter's visit but had to work on one of the days and it happened to be the day after Carter had proposed to her. She'd woken early, Carter beside her and showered without him stirring. As she dressed he looked at her and smiled. "You still want to marry me?"

"Did all of that happen last night?"

Carter lifted himself, raising his knees, a grin forming on his face, handsome despite the sleepiness of his eyes and said, "All of it, sweetheart. You haven't changed your mind have you?"

"It's all so frightening, moving so quickly. Look, I have to go. Let's discuss the practicalities when I'm back."

She leaned over him, kissing him gently on the lips, Carter drenched in her fragrance. "I'll look into what we need to do while you're busy," he said as she closed the door and left.

Chapter 3 – Summer to Autumn

Carter picked up his smartphone and searched the internet for Australian visas. It took him a few minutes to find what he was seeking. He glanced at his watch, it was almost three in the afternoon in Perth. He tapped on the phone, calling Jimmy's number. There was a pause before Jimmy answered.

"Carter, how are you. It must be early in England."

"I'm fine Jimmy, it's nearly eight. Look, I need a favour."

"Anytime, son. What is it?"

"I need you to pull some strings. I want a visa, preferably a prospective marriage one, and I need it soon. Failing that ..."

Jimmy interrupted, "Slow down, Carter, did you say prospective marriage? What you been up to, lad?"

Carter explained to a stunned Jimmy about Angie, his proposal of marriage and that he wanted to bring Angie back to Australia with him. Jimmy quizzed Carter, puzzled that his intelligent, level headed, competent personal assistant was acting so rashly. It was out of character with the Carter that he knew. Jimmy kept up the assault for half an hour, unusual for the straight speaking Lancastrian who preferred short and sharp phone conversations. "Leave it with me, lad, I'll be in touch later," was the last word of Jimmy as they broke the connection.

Jimmy was at home when he took the call from Carter, Babs in the room. She heard some of the conversation and it intrigued her so decided to stay around; this wasn't one of Jimmy's usual tedious business conversations. Jimmy's face was bedecked with confusion and concern as he placed his

Chapter 3 – Summer to Autumn

mobile phone, never far from his side, back on the coffee table. He looked at Babs and shrugged, glancing out of the six pane fold-back windows at the Olympic size swimming pool in the yard, now covered for the winter. "Spill the beans," said Babs.

Jimmy summarised the conversation he'd just had with Carter, injecting his surprise as the story unfolded. Babs listened without interrupting. She'd guessed much of it from the tone of her husband's voice during his interrogation of Carter. Jimmy finished with, "I hope he knows what he's doing?"

"Do any of us?" said Babs, smiling.

Jimmy glanced at his wife of innumerable years and his face lit up. Hadn't they done the same? They'd disappointed their family, depriving them of a big ceremony and eloped, such an old fashioned word, but representative then. They'd known each other less than three weeks. "I haven't forgotten," said Jimmy.

"He's what, thirty?"

"Twenty eight, I think," said Jimmy.

"Well, he's old enough to know what he's doing. Look, Jimmy, let me deal with this. I know some of the people in immigration, you know, when I dealt with the company's visas, let me make a few calls."

"That would help. I promised to let Carter know later today."

"Leave it with me, love."

~

Chapter 3 – Summer to Autumn

At lunch time Carter called Angie. He'd received an instant message from Babs telling him that he and Angie needed to jump on a train to London. They were to be at the Australian Embassy, in The Strand, for an appointment with one of the Ambassador's team who would provide a visa for Angie. She'd explained that the visa was expensive, but was fully paid and she'd expect it to be reimbursed when they returned and that Angie must take her passport. Angie received the message in silence and Carter had to prompt her to respond. "Jes' Carter, your rolling stone doesn't catch any moss," she said, finally.

"I'm not sure what that means," said Carter, "but I'm assuming it's positive."

When she started talking, Carter couldn't stop Angie. The life change was becoming very real, events happening faster than she could imagine. She fretted about her job, the need to tell her boss, her family, packing for the trip, a new life in Australia and the monumental journey. The furthest she'd been was Eastern Europe during her gap year. Carter interrupted, telling Angie to slow down and take things a step at a time, deciding that Angie should approach her company that afternoon and they should confront Angie's parents in the evening.

~

Dolly was with her friend on the bus, for their regular visit to the market, seated in their favourite seat. They'd been discussing Dolly's chance meeting with Irene, Angie's mother who'd been in a 'right state', as Dolly put it. Irene had told Dolly that Angie hadn't been home for a few nights but popped back, with Carter in tow, introduced him and they both

Chapter 3 – Summer to Autumn

announced that they were marrying and that Angie was moving to Australia. "It's a bit quick, they hardly know each other, marry in haste, repent at your leisure," said Betsy.

"It isn't like Angie, she's pretty level headed," said Dolly, remembering what she'd said to her when they met in the high street.

Irene had told Dolly that Carter had been grilled by Graeme, Angie's father, but that there was no shifting their position. It seemed, the more Irene and Graeme objected, the more Angie dug in her heels. Angie had asked Carter to leave so that she could speak alone to her parents. Irene said that he left reluctantly, telling her that they were a couple, they'd face adversities together. "That annoyed Irene, calling her an 'adversary', he seems to have got off on the wrong foot," said Dolly.

Irene told Dolly that, when Carter left, Angie took off the kid gloves telling her parents, leaving them in no doubt, that Carter was the one for her, that it was her decision and that she'd live with the consequences if she was wrong. She'd told them to back off and accept it because she wasn't going to change her mind. Her parents challenged Angie about leaving her well paid job and she surprised them. She'd discussed her emigration with her boss already. He'd listened and been remarkably tolerant, not wanting to lose one of his star workers to the company. He'd approached her later, after talking to his colleagues in Australia, and told her that there could be an opening for her in Sydney. Dolly had listened as Irene told her

Chapter 3 – Summer to Autumn

that Angie and Carter were in London, collecting Angie's visa and that they'd be leaving in a week.

"She's well respected at work, Irene mentioned. You know, I spoke to Angie, when I saw her get out of Carter's car. I think he comes as package. There's him, the lifestyle and the adventure of moving to Australia."

"If I was younger Dolly, I wouldn't mind unwrapping that package, he's quite a catch," said Betsy, laughing raucously.

September

Dolly was walking towards the community hall when she spotted Daniel, across the road. She waved to him and he crossed to speak to her. "How're you doing Mrs Jackson."

"I'm fine, off to a campaign meeting, you know, the bypass. How are you, now? I hear that you've been a bit off colour."

"Oh, you mean Angie and me, the break-up. I'm over that now. Just as well, as it happened. She's run off with that Australian bloke, left a week ago. I hope she knows what she's doing."

Dolly smiled, not wanting to widen the rift, nor take sides, she said, "And what about you, Daniel. You must be qualified by now."

"I'm a sparky, Mrs Jackson. My grandad lent me some money and I've bought into Y-PEC, I'm a partner, of two. I've my own van as well."

"Y-PEC?"

Chapter 3 – Summer to Autumn

"Yorkshire's Premier Electrical Contractor," said Daniel, smiling.

"Ah yes, of course. Well, you're doing grand, young man, a credit to you."

"Just off to Skipton, meeting someone," said Daniel.

"I won't hold you up, have a good time."

"I intend to," said Daniel, a grin spreading across his face.

Dolly continued on to the village hall and opened the door. Betsy was present already, in the kitchen, waving to her through the hatch. Betsy made a gesture and Dolly nodded, confirming that she'd like a cup of tea. The bypass campaign team consisted of twelve members, including Irene, Angie's mother, who was talking to Beatrice as Dolly collected her drink. Angie was the topic on everyone's lips and Dolly wondered whether Angie's ears were burning, wherever she was in her epic journey in life. Later, Irene confirmed that Angie and Carter were in Perth, Angie having made a trip to Sydney for an interview for a position with her old company there, successful as it happened, Carter and Angie were to be married in a couple of weeks, then they were moving permanently to Sydney as Carter's job was changing too. Irene had become sanguine, the initial incredulity and anger passing. Inside, Dolly was amused, for it seemed to her that Angie had deprived her mother of a glorious wedding, seemingly irritating her more than her daughter emigrating.

"They don't waste time," Beatrice said, secretly impressed by the couple taking hold of life's chances, as she and Ambrose

Chapter 3 – Summer to Autumn

had done many years earlier. She then brought the meeting to order to discuss campaign tactics. The outcome was radical, leaving Dolly uncomfortable as she glanced over at Betsy, who winked and smiled.

~

They seemed to appear in an instant. The High Street was festooned with banners proclaiming the need for a bypass for Heythwaite bearing the catchy slogan 'No truck, Heythwaite demands a bypass'. The rebuilt bus stop, the scene of the disaster, was plastered with photographs of the incident with the articulated lorry, plus 'No Truck' posters. Beatrice's press contacts were compliant and she was interviewed on many of the local radio stations and for articles in the local press. She was perfect, her cultured accent, embellished by a hint of Yorkshire dialect, resonated with listeners: educated but still 'one of us'. Their next stunt made the regional news, and then went national. Early on a warm Friday morning, helped by local farmers, the road was blocked as a pen was built hurriedly, then filled with Alastair's Wensleydale sheep. Two tractors were parked across the road, fore and aft, to prevent traffic from ploughing into the sheep. Protesters, mostly women, many from the campaign team, stood in front of the tractors brandishing placards. The traffic stopped and then started to queue. Soon, the line backed up to the top of the hill, blocking it, so that all roads into and out of Heythwaite were snarled. Within a half hour, the police arrived to take control and the media landed a helicopter in one of Alastair's fields. News of the protest spread to the local networks, the BBC and

Chapter 3 – Summer to Autumn

Independent regional news. Later, footage would be shown on the twenty four hour news channels and then the evening news. The sight of septuagenarians being hustled into the back of police cars was soon seen by millions around the world on social media. It took two hours for the police to clear the road and a further three before the traffic was moving smoothly again.

~

Dolly and Betsy were in the Old Oak pub, Dolly cradling a large brandy. They didn't frequent the ale house often but, on this occasion, 'needs must'. They'd both been active in the demonstration, holding high their signs, affixed to wooden poles. The police had been gentle with them and they'd escaped with a conditional caution, provided they cause no further affrays. After the experience, Dolly was sure that she didn't wish to repeat the experience. Betsy wasn't so certain, now attached to the notion of direct action and people power. Beatrice had been kept for longer and had appeared at a hastily convened magistrates court and given a conditional discharge. She was happy to accept the terms; her view was there was no need to repeat the stunt for their point had been made and the publicity invaluable. Ambrose had collected her after the hearing and her smiling face and waving hand, from the passenger seat of their silver BMW, appeared on the front page of the local rag.

Bert and Walter joined the two ladies at their table, Bert asking, "You want another, Dolly, Betsy?"

Chapter 3 – Summer to Autumn

"Don't mind if I do, mine's a half of Theakston's Old Peculiar," said Betsy.

"Not for me, thanks Bert, this is more than enough," said Dolly glancing at her glass of spirit.

Bert walked to the bar, placed his order and returned to Dolly, Betsy and Walter, saying, "Nancy's going to bring them over."

"How're you two doing?" said Walter, "You've created quite a rumpus by all accounts. Daniel tells me you're all over Facebook and Twitter, whatever they are, as well as the news. The picture of you two being manhandled into the police car is a classic."

"We were treated well," said Dolly, "Certainly not manhandled, Walter."

Walter smiled as he said, "Well, you've placed Heythwaite on the map and highlighted the campaign. Well done, ladies."

"Not everyone wants a bypass," said Bert, "Especially the shops in the High Street. They think they'll lose business."

"Oh, they always say that," said Walter.

"I hear Beatrice was charged and then bound over to keep the peace," said Bert.

"She was, dear," said Dolly, "I don't think we'll need a rerun so that should be easy for her."

"Oh, I enjoyed it. Haven't felt this good since you and me went to Australia, Dolly, when you clobbered that bloke," said Betsy, chuckling.

Chapter 3 – Summer to Autumn

Nancy arrived with their drinks, her manner frosty towards the ladies as she said, "Old Peculiar for you Betsy, your usual Bert, Walter. No Harold this evening?"

"At Dora's sister in Harrogate," said Bert.

"He'll pay a few bob more for a pint there," said Nancy as she left.

"Something's amiss with Nancy," said Betsy, "You'd need a pick to break that ice."

"She doesn't support your campaign, Betsy," said Bert, "Thinks you should focus on better parking so that people can stop at her pub."

"If she'd seen that accident happen, perhaps she'd think differently," said Dolly.

~

Daniel was walking his mother's dog, a border collie, five years of age and full of energy. He was taking a footpath across Alastair's farm when he heard an irritating buzzing noise. Buster, the dog, heard it too and started barking, jumping up and down. Daniel looked up and spotted the drone, heading for Heythwaite, sweeping across the sky as the wind caught it. He glanced around, looking for the drone's operator but saw nobody. It had been a regular occurrence in the sky around Heythwaite and was becoming a nuisance; it wasn't clear who was controlling it and what they were doing with the images they'd obtained. An idea was formulating in Daniel's mind.

~

Chapter 3 – Summer to Autumn

Amy had badgered Alistair into visiting the new optician in Heythwaite. She'd watched him squinting, even when wearing his glasses. It had been seven years since his last eye test and Amy was concerned, especially with Alastair operating farm machinery. He walked through the Optician's door, smelling the freshness of new paint and the refurbishment. Behind a light oak coloured reception desk was seated a young lady with shoulder length blond hair, smart grey uniform and her face embellished with turquoise rimmed varifocal spectacles. "Mr Shaw, is it?" she said and Alastair nodded, "Gareth will be with you in a moment, please take a seat."

Alastair looked at the line of new chairs with their aquamarine coloured covers, facing away from the shop window, and took a seat next to the attached low table, upon which were today's newspapers. Seated, he thumbed through the Yorkshire Post. It was difficult to avoid articles about the 'civil disobedience', as the press had called it. Beatrice's photograph was everywhere, embellishing articles where she was quoted verbatim. She was certainly achieving publicity for the cause. Alastair had managed to escape arrest as the police were more concerned about him moving the tractor and livestock so that they could clear the road.

"Mr Shaw," said Gareth.

"Alastair, call me Alastair."

Gareth grinned as he spotted what Alastair was reading and said, "I thought that I was moving to a quiet rural location!"

"You have, lad. It's normally quiet around here. What've you done to yourself?" Alastair had noticed that Gareth was

Chapter 3 – Summer to Autumn

sporting a plaster cast from his ankle to just above the knee and was walking with crutches.

"Rugby," said Gareth as Alastair nodded.

"Not great timing," said Alastair, "What with you just opening."

"You're right," said Gareth, "Julia, my wife, is livid. Self inflicted, she tells me."

"Are you going to be able to manage?"

"It's awkward, but I'll be fine. The only problem is that I have a few weeks with this cast," said Gareth, pointing towards his practice room with his free hand.

Alastair walked past Gareth into the surgery as Gareth hobbled after him. Seated, Gareth started his wizardry, placing a contraption on the bridge of Alastair's nose allowing different lenses to be trialled. Alastair peered at the large, then progressively smaller letters on a screen at the far end of the room as Gareth completed tests that would allow him to asses the prescription needed by the farmer. During the session, Gareth chatted to Alastair, asking him about the farm, family and life. Gareth's warm manner allowed Alastair to open himself up in a way that he hadn't for some time. After a physical examination of Alastair's eyes, Gareth performed a peripheral vision test for each eye, followed by a blast of air to check for glaucoma. Gareth looked at his notes, discovering that Alastair had not consulted an optician for seven years, so suggested an Optical Coherence Tomography, or OCT, examination, one that would photograph the inside of the eye,

Chapter 3 – Summer to Autumn

providing a cross section of the retina, diagnosing any issues. Gareth told Alastair that there would be an additional charge for the inspection and the thrifty farmer almost faltered but, after looking at Gareth, decided to continue. It was a wise decision, for Gareth found a small pool of fluid in Alastair's left eye, interfering with the function of the retina. Patiently, Gareth showed Alastair the photos that he'd taken and the area of fluid, away from the centre of the eye where its impact would have been more obvious to Alastair, but still significant; he would need to see an eye consultant, and soon. The condition was treatable, provided it didn't continue to worsen. Later, Alastair would ponder about the dark horseshoe shaped patch that he saw briefly, when he opened his left eye in the half light, as he awoke to look at the clock. Alastair was a robust Yorkshireman, not prone to fretting, but this revelation made him anxious. The prospect of blindness was something that frightened him; how would he care for the farm and his family? That possibility was now too close for comfort.

~

Betsy stepped into Edwina's Coffee House first, followed closely by Dolly, and headed for their usual table. Edwina spotted them and waved, shouting over, asking if they wanted their regular order. Dolly, waving back, confirmed that they did as they settled at the table. It had taken them nearly an hour to reach the café as they walked from Dolly's house up the High Street, something that would normally have taken a few minutes. TV crews covering the demonstration that closed the main road in Heythwaite linked Dolly with the incident in

Chapter 3 – Summer to Autumn

Kings Park, Perth, Australia. A perfect human angle for the story, they thought and they invited Dolly to an interview on morning television. Reluctant initially, Beatrice persuaded Dolly that the publicity would be wonderful for the campaign. Betsy accompanied Dolly to Manchester for the interview and they were collected in a chauffeur driven Mercedes for the two and a half hour journey to the studio. Watching from the wings, Betsy marvelled as Dolly was interviewed. The presenter attempted to demolish Dolly's arguments, associating her aggression in Perth with the civil disobedience of the bypass campaign. Dolly refused to let the interviewer irk her. Dolly's natural 'niceness' was the winning trait at the end of the short interview, transmitted live to the TV audience. By the time they arrived back in Heythwaite, Dolly was a star and everyone wanted to talk to her. That's why the journey to Edwina's had taken so long.

"You did well, made that presenter look like an evil witch," said Edwina, placing on the table a tray containing teapot, milk in a jug, two cups and saucers, a plate containing a cherry bakewell and one with a large slice of battenburg cake.

"Oh, I don't think so, dear. I just told her what needed to be said."

"Beatrice was in earlier. She's delighted, like the cat that got the cream, if you ask me. It'll do that campaign for a bypass some good," said Edwina.

Initially, Edwina expressed reservations about the bypass, worried that she'd lose business from passing trade. She'd rationalised that parking was so difficult in Heythwaite that

Chapter 3 – Summer to Autumn

little of her takings came from strangers and had switched her support to the campaign. She'd seen how Dolly had been affected by the accident and how long Dick had taken to recover and that had impacted her opinion. Mostly, she'd seen the detached attitude of the County Council in public meetings, mimicking the government's line that 'there was no magic money tree'. She knew that, when money was needed for some pet project, or for some political expedient, the tree would bear fruit. Now was the time for it to deliver for Heythwaite and she admired the campaign team for their inventive approach. "Did you know that Amanda Braithwaite wanted to second Beatrice onto the Town Council, with Angie swanning off to Australia," said Betsy.

"Yes, I had heard that. Turned them down, didn't she?" said Edwina.

"Conflict of interest, dear," said Dolly, "It would be difficult for her to lobby for a bypass and stand as an impartial councillor."

"It's a pity. She's the type who gets things done," said Edwina, peering over the top of her spectacles.

"Unlike Amanda, who likes to be in the right place at the right time," said Betsy.

"Talking of the council," said Edwina, subtly changing the subject, "Have you heard from Angie?"

"Last I heard, dear, was that Angie and Carter were married, a small affair, just a few close friends, and they've moved to Sydney," said Dolly.

Chapter 3 – Summer to Autumn

"All rather quick," said Edwina.

"Young love," said Dolly, smiling.

"Well, I hope it lasts," said Betsy.

~

With the last breath of summer came the 'old folks outing' to the coast, Scarborough this year. Fourteen pensioners had signed up for the trip, the majority from Heythwaite and a group from a nearby village. The morning was cool, a heavy dew soaking the grass verge, but the day promised sunshine with a few clouds and warmth. The aroma of autumn was in the air but summer was reluctant to leave. Dolly and Betsy were first in the queue opposite the bus stop, Walter with them. Harold and Dora were holidaying in Bridlington, along the coast from Scarborough so wouldn't join the outing but Bert and Elsie were expected. Annie, Daniel's grandmother, walked towards the bus stop with Madge, the hairdresser, greeted others in the queue and joined at the rear. Walter's phone rang as the minibus came around the corner and he looked at its screen. It was Bert ringing and he answered the call. Dolly looked on anxiously as Walter listened, his face twisting, the call causing him discomfort. The bus pulled up at the stop and the door folded open. Betsy walked onto the bus, followed by Dolly as Walter stepped aside to allow other passengers to alight. Betsy selected the second row of seats on the right, seating herself by the window. Dolly shuffled in beside her. Finishing the call, Walter was the last on the bus, leaning towards the driver to speak to him. The driver opened some papers and made an annotation on the page as Walter walked

Chapter 3 – Summer to Autumn

over to Dolly and Betsy. "Is everything all right, dear?" said Dolly, leaning over.

"Bert and Elsie aren't going to be able to make it. He's at the hospital, accident and emergency."

"Oh, my, what's happened?"

"Elsie said that he came over queer, faint and dizzy, heart beating oddly and pains in his chest."

"When? This morning, I suppose?" said Betsy, stepping up to look over the top of the seat."

"Must have been, I didn't ask. I'm going to stay here, find out how Bert's doing, pop over to the hospital later. He'll be mad, they enjoy this trip."

As Walter stepped down from the bus and made his way along the High Street, the bus driver walked to the back of the bus, then meandered towards the front, checking his inventory of passengers, ticking the sheet to confirm that everyone was on board. Satisfied, he took his position at the front, turned the ignition key and closed the door. Engine labouring, the old bus drifted into the road, up the High Street and turned at the top of the hill, setting a route for the coast. Betsy glanced at Dolly as she said, "This vehicle is as old as us, hope we make it."

~

Edwina watched the minibus struggle up the hill and turned away from the window as it disappeared from sight. She'd wanted to go on the outing but Jane, her assistant, couldn't work Wednesdays, so Edwina needed to be at the café. Watching the stream of black smoke belching from the exhaust,

Chapter 3 – Summer to Autumn

Edwina wondered if she'd made the right call after all. The 'ding' of the door bell caught her attention and she turned to see who had entered. Gareth stood in the doorway, negotiating his way through as he hobbled on his crutch, holding his cast encased left leg off the ground. Edwina rushed forward to help Gareth but he shook his head, saying with a gentle West Yorkshire, accent, "It's okay, I'm getting used to them."

"You're Gareth, aren't you, the optician?"

"Yes, and you must be Edwina, as in 'Edwina's Coffee House'."

Edwina smiled as she showed Gareth to a table, near the door. She glanced at the optician, pleased that a young family had moved into the village. Guessing he was in his thirties she quizzed him about his wife and offspring. He chatted, bereft of inhibitions sometimes prevalent among professional classes, telling Edwina about his children, two boys and a girl aged ten, eight and seven respectively, and his spouse Julia, a doctor who worked in Skipton. The morning had been fraught for Gareth, who'd had to attend to the school run, difficult in his condition. Unusually, Julia had been forced to work an overnight shift because of staff sickness. Breakfast was in order before he started his day at ten, when his business opened. He ordered a bacon roll, plus a large Americano with hot milk.

"You're on the campaign committee, aren't you," said Edwina as she delivered Gareth's breakfast.

"The bypass, yes, it seemed like a way to integrate into the community."

Chapter 3 – Summer to Autumn

"Judging by the look on your face, it hasn't quite worked out like that."

Gareth explained that he'd been one of a few voices against the road closure stunt and he'd refused to be involved in it. He explained that Dolly had also spoken against the idea but had still turned out and contributed. "I think I lost some credibility, especially as a newcomer."

Edwina glanced into the blue grey eyes of Gareth as he ran his fingers through his thinning blond hair and said, "They'll get over it. It seemed to do the trick, gaining a lot of publicity. Last I heard, the stunt swayed the Town and District Council, not sure if the County Council is taking it seriously."

"There's an election next year, that might have an impact."

"We'll see, enjoy your breakfast," said Edwina as she walked away from the table.

~

Walter's phone rang at eleven o'clock as he was walking from the hospital after visiting Bert. He'd told the ward staff that he was Bert's brother so that he could see Bert as only close relatives were permitted entry. As he was of Caribbean origin, nobody believed him but he was allowed access. Bert was feeling better and Elsie informed Walter that Bert had regained some of his colour and that she'd been anxious for him. A consultant had seen Bert and examined the ECG that a junior doctor had requisitioned when Bert was admitted. His diagnosis was that Bert's heart was suffering arrhythmias and that he'd probably need a pacemaker fitting. Further tests had

Chapter 3 – Summer to Autumn

been ordered by the consultant and Bert would remain in hospital for a few days. Walter fumbled for the phone in his pocket, a hand-me-down from his nephew and a simple device, with few frills. He punched the 'answer' button and put the phone to his ear.

"Walter, it's Dolly. Have you heard from Bert?"

Walter told Dolly that he'd seen Bert and explained the consultant's prognosis, as he understood it. Dolly sympathised but could do little else.

"How's Scarborough?" said Walter.

"Bit brisk, but the sun's out and it's warm where it's sheltered," said Dolly, "We're all meeting up for lunch at the fish restaurant. Annie, you know, Daniel's grandmother, is with us and we're going to do a bit of promenading before we eat."

The bus had dropped the pensioners by Luna Park, a small fun-fair, near the pier. Annie had moved forward on the bus when she heard about Bert and had decided to tag along with Betsy and Dolly. The tide was in and little of Scarborough's famous stretch of golden sand was visible. Betsy suggested that they walk along the pier, towards the yacht club; the view of Scarborough and the castle on the top of the hill was superb from there, she'd said. Betsy's assessment was spot-on, the coastal vista opening up before them like a painting, hills and castle as a backdrop, layered with tiers of terracotta and slate roofed buildings and a foreground of the green-grey north sea, dotted with berthed fishing vessels. At the end of the pier was a new addition to Scarborough's entertainment industry. A large poster promised 'The Thrill of a Jet Boat Ride' around the

Chapter 3 – Summer to Autumn

harbour. It didn't have the splendour of the Shotover Gorge near Queenstown in New Zealand, where an accompanying photograph was taken, but it spiked Annie's interest and she suggested the ride to Betsy and Dolly. Dolly wasn't sure and took a little persuading but Betsy was game, after all, she'd been to Australia which was near New Zealand, wasn't it?

"Are you sure we have time?" was Dolly's last attempt at resisting before the three old ladies climbed down the concrete steps, Dolly gripping the handrail, towards the awaiting purpose built boat. It was propelled by a fast moving jet of water, making it supremely manoeuvrable, something the pensioners would discover soon. Betsy stepped confidently onto the craft, helping Dolly, close behind, as she lifted her legs and placed them tentatively on the floor of the boat. Aided by a young assistant, Annie was next and the three were soon seated in the middle of the three rows. The ride filled quickly, mostly with students, renegades from college, each passenger donning a life jacket. An athletic looking driver, who introduced himself as Nigel, took the front seat, activated a pre-recorded safety briefing and then started the powerful motor that roared into life. A stream of water drifted from the rear of the vessel as it moved forwards and then turned towards the centre of the harbour. "Oh, it's not too bad," said Dolly, smiling at Betsy.

In the middle channel Nigel opened up the motor and a powerful jet gushed behind them, angry, turbulent and white. The front of the craft lifted as Dolly gripped the rail in front of her, closing her eyes for a moment, swallowing hard. That was just the start. Nigel swept around in a tight circle and diamonds

Chapter 3 – Summer to Autumn

of water leapt into the air as the vessel lurched into the turn. First one way, then the next, the jet boat traced a tight figure of eight within the harbour walls, watched by hoards of onlookers, the best advertisement for the ride as it attracted howls of wonder. Dolly screeched involuntarily at each turn; there was little opportunity to converse, noise, continual change of direction and the rush of water prevented it. As a climax to the ride, Nigel headed for the harbour wall and the wail of passengers could be heard as the vessel came closer. Nigel had done this countless times and, with consummate skill, spun the boat around, circled twice and cut the engine to a purr. He then plotted a course for the harbour steps and moored, ready for the next trip. Betsy looked at her friend who's pallor had taken on a creamy colour. "Are you alright?"

Dolly was about to answer when one of the students in the seats in front turned his head and said to the three pensioners, "Hey ladies, you're cool. Can't imagine my gran doing this. Right on."

He turned away again as Dolly whispered, "I will be, when I'm back on dry land."

~

Edwina was locking up the café when the minibus turned the corner, stopped and spilled the group of garrulous pensioners onto the pavement. Annie was grinning as she said goodbye to Dolly and Betsy, tapping Betsy on the arm in a conspiratorial manner and then laughing. Edwina stepped towards the day-trippers as Annie was leaving and she exchanged small talk with her before Annie scuttled away.

Chapter 3 – Summer to Autumn

"How was your day?"

"Fabulous," said Betsy.

"They tried to kill me," said Dolly, a twinkle in her eye.

"You'll have to explain that one," said Edwina, tipping her head to one side, incomprehension sweeping across her face.

The ride still fresh in Betsy's mind, Edwina felt the thrill by proxy as Betsy described the jet boat trip around the harbour. "What you girls get up to. You'll be climbing Everest next," said Edwina, looking up at something in the sky.

"Don't give her ideas, dear," said Dolly.

"There's that damn drone again, it's a nuisance, something should be done about it. Have you heard about Bert," said Edwina, looking up at the aircraft for a moment. Dolly told Edwina of her earlier conversation with Walter. Edwina had no additional news, hearing the same tale from Walter when he'd called in for his lunch.

"You're late closing," said Dolly.

"I had some paperwork to do. I haven't finished it but said I'd meet Walter in the Old Oak, want to join us?"

Betsy glanced at Dolly who smiled as Betsy said, "It would finish off the day, as long as we're not gooseberries."

Edwina laughed and shook her head as she said, "I think you'd better come, if only to stop Heythwaite gossiping."

~

Daniel was studying the circuit diagram that he'd obtained from the internet, annotated with his own modifications. He had all of the components that he needed, mostly scrounged, including a powerful radio transmitter, microphone, parabolic dish, servo motors for steering and miscellaneous components. The mechanical work was complete and his design would scan the sky, look for the tell-tale signature noise of the drone and lock on to it, then pulse the transmitter to confuse the radio control of the craft, bringing it down. Only the electronic wizardry needed completing and then he'd test it. He spun the axle of the servo motors and watched as the dish rotated; it would scan the sky in a series of arcs, controlled by a hobby computer, the missing piece of his contraption.

Chapter 4 – Autumn to Winter

October

Briefly, the Indian summer trickled into October but, as the days shortened, the nights became cooler and the leaves began to lose their chlorophyll, browning at the edges in the wind and then taking on a yellow hue. The summer broke with a storm of biblical proportions. Dolly had slept fitfully, the sound of thunder rumbling around the valley and the rain pounding relentlessly against the window, bouncing from the conservatory roof. She woke with a start as an explosive 'crash' sound filled the heavens, shaking the house. She arose from her bed, donned a dressing gown, descended the stairs and checked around the house, finding that everything was in order. Outside, the storm raged, the cloudburst continuing, causing water to flow down the hill like a river. The sky was dark with sullen clouds, lightning streaking across them followed closely by the boom-boom-boom of the thunder. Dolly looked at the clock in the kitchen as she filled the kettle and placed it on the stove. It was six thirty in the morning, little different to the normal time that she'd wake. As Dolly added tea leaves to the pot she heard the sound of sirens so rushed to the front window to witness a fire engine, followed by a police car, climb the High Street. The sky had taken on an orange tinge and wisps of smoke circled in the gusty wind. The kettle started its whistle to indicate that it was boiling, so Dolly returned to the kitchen to finish making the tea. Whilst letting it brew, after pouring milk into her white china mug, she returned

Chapter 4 – Autumn to Winter

to the window. The glow was brighter, barely masked by the coming dawn dulled by the relentless storm. Dolly fetched her tea and returned to her lookout point as a policeman, wearing a mackintosh, head down in the torrential wind and rain, trudged towards her house after knocking on a neighbours door. Placing her cup on the coffee table, she walked to the door, opening it before the constable knocked. "Is there something wrong?" Dolly said as she pulled open the door against a gust of wind.

"The Co-operative store has been struck by lightning," he said, shouting against the noise of the storm, "It's on fire and we may have to evacuate if the fire spreads. The brigade think they have it under control and this rain is helping them. As a precaution, could you ready yourself, just in case, you know, get dressed, pack a few essentials?"

Retrieving her cup from the table, Dolly walked upstairs, washed and dressed in record time, using only a small amount of make-up, and then brushed her hair. As she descended the stairs, the telephone rang. "Dolly, it's Betsy. Are you alright? I've just heard about the lightning strike on the Co-op."

"I'm fine, Betsy. There's a commotion in the High Street, must be three fire engines. A policeman's just called, said something about evacuating us. I'm far enough away from the Co-op, I doubt if it will be necessary, especially in this torrent."

The ground shook and windows rattled; Dolly heard the sound of a blast as the sky lit up with a yellow glow. "What was that, I heard it from here," said Betsy.

"I don't know, dear, but whatever it was, it's serious."

Chapter 4 – Autumn to Winter

Further up the hill, Edwina, hearing the lightning strike, had dressed quickly and checked her coffee house, fearing the worst. Relieved that there was no damage to her premises, she tuned to the local radio station and listened to reports about a fire in Heythwaite being tackled by the fire service with an evacuation being considered. The news reporter told of a thunderbolt hitting the Co-operative store in the High Street. Edwina was across the road and some distance from it, so doubted if she'd be impacted. She made herself a cup of coffee, waiting for the next bulletin from the radio programme, it reverting to playing music in the interim. The rain was teeming, storm-force wind causing it to pound against the window, turbulence making the water swirl as if the window was being cleaned. Edwina hoped that she would not have to abandon her café, especially in the storm. Gazing down the hill, she could make out three fire engines and two police cars, their pulsating lights pinpointing their position in the half light of dawn, made darker by the menacing clouds. A flicker of flames came from the Co-op, a yellow glow betraying the devastation within. The blast was sudden, causing the door to tremble and the windows buckle, springing back as the pressure wave streaked up the hill. From her vantage point, Edwina watched as a flash of orange opened up the roof of the store and flames leapt into the air. The storm, bringer of adversity, was also a saviour. As the rain intensified it quenched the flames, aided by the valiant efforts of the fire brigade. By daylight, the fire was out, but all that remained of the Co-operative and the newsagent next door was a burned out shell.

Chapter 4 – Autumn to Winter

~

Gareth had to park on the outskirts of Heythwaite again as traffic was at a standstill; police had created a makeshift contraflow system whilst the emergency services finished their work and it was slowing traffic. The storm had blown over but the rain remained and Gareth was drenched by the time he reached his opticians, on the opposite side of the High Street, well away from the charred remains of the Co-op. He'd heard the news on the radio and was anxious to discover if there'd been any damage to his practice. His way was blocked by a policeman and Gareth explained to him that his premises were up the hill from the incident. Allowed to pass, Gareth entered his opticians, and was reassured by what he found. There'd been no damage, only the smell of smoke that pervaded the whole area. The inundation from the tempest had prevented a worse tragedy but it was unlikely that many of his patients would make it to see him today. He checked the diary on his smartphone; the day was meant to be busy. As he was examining the calendar the phone rang and it startled him; the display told him that his receptionist was calling. Gareth answered and she explained that she was trapped in the traffic mayhem and would be late. The surgery telephone rang so Gareth terminated the mobile phone conversation and lifted the receiver.

"Heythwaite Opticians," said Gareth.

"I've an appointment in half an hour," said the male voice on the other end, "There's some kind of hubbub going on so I'll be a little late, maybe five minutes."

Chapter 4 – Autumn to Winter

"That's okay, make it when you can. There's been a big fire in the town. I think today might be a challenge," said Gareth.

"Looks like it, see you soon," said the caller.

The door opened as Gareth put down the phone and Beatrice walked through and smiled at Gareth as she shook her brolly outside. "My, that's a mess out there. I'm a little early," she said but Gareth seemed preoccupied so she added, "My eye inspection. This is the right day, isn't it?"

"Beatrice, yes, sorry. My receptionist is caught in the mayhem, she'll be in soon but I'm on my own at the moment."

"Well, it could have been worse."

"You mean, the fire, yes, we've been lucky," said Gareth.

"Actually, I meant that you no longer have your plaster cast. How is it, by the way?"

"Ah, I see. Yes, that is a blessing. It's fine, a bit of muscle waste but that'll improve now I'm mobile again. Please, go through to the consulting room, I'll be with you shortly. I'll just leave a note on the counter, explaining for the next patient."

Gareth wrote on letter headed paper 'Please take a seat, I'll be with you shortly. The incident in the High Street is impacting us.' and stuck it to the rear of the computer screen. He joined Beatrice and, as he closed the door, said, "How's Ambrose, it's a while since I've seen him."

The receptionist didn't make it in that day, nor many of Gareth's clients, especially those who lived outside of Heythwaite, south of the river Wharfe. Shortly after Beatrice arrived for her appointment, the police stopped traffic

Chapter 4 – Autumn to Winter

travelling over the bridge spanning the river at the foot of the hill. The Wharfe was swollen, almost to the top of its banks, but that wasn't their concern. The section above the central support for two of the arches of the bridge had developed a crack that was widening. Police feared that the bridge would collapse into the raging torrent of the Wharfe, notably because the height of the river was above the archway. Traffic flow ceased, the nearest river crossing suitable for heavier traffic was twelve miles to the east. Far away from Heythwaite, vehicles were being diverted, leaving a convoy of cars and lorries stuck with nowhere to go. Cars, their drivers impatient of waiting, pulled out of the queue, performing dangerous u-turns in poor visibility, clogging up the smaller routes, mostly single track roads, with passing places. Traffic snarled to a standstill in a wide circle around Heythwaite.

~

The following day the weather, as if embarrassed at what it had inflicted, turned demure. The sun shone, temperatures rose, fluffy clouds littered the sky and a light westerly breeze blew. It was difficult to imagine the turmoil of the previous day unless one looked around. Trees had been stripped of their leaves, some losing boughs, the major store of the town had been reduced to ashes and the newsagent was a blackened shell. Coupled, an uncanny silence pervaded Heythwaite. There's an old saying that reads 'its an ill wind that blows no one any good' and Beatrice intended to capitalise on Heythwaite's misfortune. The Wharfe remained in flood and the central bridge support had developed a wide fissure. The

Chapter 4 – Autumn to Winter

Highways Department of the County Council had closed the bridge, sending consultants to examine it. They were busy performing inspections from both banks and the road leading from Heythwaite. A TV crew were observing, cameras ready but not rolling. A crunching sound, followed by a rumble from the bridge caused them to leap into action. Soon, a television audience was to witness the collapse of the central column and a yellow hatted engineer in a high visibility vest scramble desperately up the bank to escape the bough wave that followed as the bridge fell into the River Wharfe, making the southern road into Heythwaite unusable. Beatrice, who was watching in awe, gathered herself together, spotting an opportunity. As the camera swung around, surveying the devastation she caught the eye of a news reporter and nodded to him. Eloquently, she told a tale of the maelstrom of the storm, thunderbolt that caused the fire and then wove the collapse of the bridge into a plea for a bypass, the implication being that the God's had spoken. By the evening, most people in the region, then nationally, knew of Heythwaite's plight, the bridge disintegration and Beatrice's interview, distributed liberally. Questions were being asked of County Councillors, then local Members of Parliament and finally Ministers of the Government. Within two days, resistance collapsed and the Government agreed to provide the funds for the bypass and the County Council capitulated too.

Betsy was with Dolly at Dolly's house when the telephone rang; it was Beatrice calling, "Beatrice, dear. I saw your interview, then the Minister, then the County Council. It's unbelievable, we are to have our bypass. Well done."

Chapter 4 – Autumn to Winter

"I was in the right place at the right time," said Beatrice, "It's not over Dolly. We need to keep up the pressure. Once the spotlight's off us, they'll revert to form. I'm suggesting that we create a smaller central committee from our campaign team to maintain momentum. I'm calling everyone to see what they think."

"And, what do people think?"

"I'm about half of the way through. I've had no objection so far. I wondered if you and Betsy would be part of the smaller group?"

Dolly told Beatrice that she was with Betsy, explained to Betsy what Beatrice had said and asked for Betsy's views before returning to Beatrice, saying, "We'd be delighted, Beatrice. How many were you thinking of inviting?"

"Only a few. Yourselves, Irene and Gareth, the optician, I was thinking. How does that sound?"

"Plus yourself, dear."

"Of course, I would like to continue the campaign," said Beatrice, the inflection in her voice betraying that she was smiling.

"We couldn't have achieved this without you, Beatrice."

After exchanging chit-chat and retelling the turmoil of the last few days they terminated the call, Dolly returning to Betsy to continue the topic they were discussing prior to Beatrice's call.

"You were saying that Bert is home and he's had a pacemaker fitted, dear," said Dolly.

Chapter 4 – Autumn to Winter

"Elsie told me. He came home just before that storm. She said that he'd been a bit queer for a while, wouldn't see the doctor of course. Tired, irritable at times she told me. Anyhow, he had this turn, breathless and an awful colour, Elsie said. That's when they found that his heart wasn't beating properly. The consultant told Bert that he needed a pacemaker and that was that."

"How is he now?" said Dolly.

"Better, by all accounts. He's a bit conscious of it at the moment but Elsie said that you can hardly see where it is. He's having a check-up in a few weeks and then every six months."

"He'll find being stuck in the house a bind," said Dolly.

"Elsie's barred him from the allotment and the pub until his next hospital visit. It hasn't gone down well."

"I bet it hasn't, dear."

~

With the southern exit of Heythwaite, at the bottom of the hill, closed to traffic, the bus to Wednesday's Skipton Market had to make a detour and took fifteen minutes longer. As usual, Betsy and Dolly were waiting at the bus stop as the bus turned the corner and halted. "Morning, Mrs Longbottom, this is all a bit of a mess isn't it?" said Hamid, grinning.

Betsy placed her pass on the reader and removed it when she heard the 'beep' sound, saying, "It's been awful, we're almost cut off."

"The company has had to change the timetable as well, it's causing chaos," said Hamid.

Chapter 4 – Autumn to Winter

"Better get used to it young man. It'll be a while before the bridge is fixed," Betsy replied, then walked down the bus, making for their usual seat. Dolly entered the bus next, speaking briefly to Hamid before joining Betsy. The bus drifted forward, stopped, reversed around a corner and returned the way it had arrived, now unable to exit over the bridge. The morning had a touch of autumn, a musty smell hung in the still air, and a fine mist dampened the spirit and the body. As Hamid drove up the hill, Dolly wiped the condensation away from the window and glanced out of the bus. The High Street was eerily quiet, with few vehicles venturing out, only the odd delivery van. She pondered, wondering if it would be like this once the bypass had been built. Qualms were developing until a vision of the lorry demolishing the bus shelter materialised in her mind, followed by that of Dick, prostrate and pasty looking, being loaded into the ambulance. She shook her head, sure that they were fighting the right battle.

"Are you alright, Dolly, you seem distracted," said Betsy.

"Oh, just looking at the High Street, dear."

"It'll be back to normal in no time," said Betsy, "Those two Polish workmen are back too, working on the Co-op store. I saw them this morning."

"Alex and Iggy, yes, Edwina was telling me. I think they like working in Heythwaite. Well, there's plenty of work for them at present."

"That there is," said Betsy, who then changed the subject, "Have you heard about Alastair? I was speaking to Amy the

Chapter 4 – Autumn to Winter

other day, that lad of hers is growing, sitting up in the pram he was."

"Is he, I haven't seen Amy, she doesn't seem to leave the farm. What's this about Alastair?"

Betsy told Dolly that Alastair had seen Gareth, the optician, who'd told Alastair that he had some problem with the retina. Gareth had referred Alastair to a hospital consultant, who he was seeing in November. Amy had told Betsy that Alastair was worried about going blind.

"She told him that he might have done if he hadn't seen Gareth," said Betsy, "It was Amy who forced him to go. You know what farmers are like, tight as they come."

"Is there a risk of him losing his sight? I don't know how Alastair would cope with that," said Dolly.

"Apparently, Gareth told Alastair that it could be treated," said Betsy.

"Well, that's a blessing, dear," said Dolly, looking forward as the bus turned into a narrow lane.

"Where you going Hamid?" shouted Betsy, "This isn't the normal route. Are you kidnapping us?"

"Why would I do that, you're not worth anything," said Hamid, laughing, "I'm picking up at some of the other villages Mrs Longbottom, since the timetable changed."

"Well, the road looks narrower than the bus, if you ask me," said Betsy, glancing at Dolly.

Chapter 4 – Autumn to Winter

The wet autumnal vegetation of the verge brushed up against the bus on both sides as Hamid drove along the narrow twisty lane, passing wider spots intended to allow vehicles coming in the opposite direction to cross each other. He stopped at several hamlets on the way to pick up passengers no longer served by other services since the bridge collapsed in Heythwaite. At the opening to a field, a tractor and trailer started to inch out of the gate and Hamid gave a short hoot of the horn, letting the farmer know that they were there. The tractor halted, allowing Hamid to drive by, towards a sharp left turn, easing the bus around the corner. Dolly breathed in sharply and looked at Betsy who had her hands over her eyes in mock horror. The bus stopped abruptly as another tractor, bereft of trailer, came into view, followed by a lorry and two cars. Behind the bus was the earlier tractor who had followed Hamid along the road. Opening the bus door, Hamid called up to the driver of the farm vehicle, asking him to reverse. He jumped down from the tractor, trudged along the road and approached the drivers of the truck and cars behind him. The convoy reversed in slow motion, the bus following in their wake, until they reached the cross roads, a mile and a half from the bend, where the bus was due to turn. Free of his confinement, Hamid stepped on the accelerator and they sped towards Skipton.

Leaning forwards, Betsy shouted, "That was exciting, Hamid."

"It's impossible, Mrs Longbottom. The pen pushers have no idea when it comes to routes, none at all," said Hamid, exhaling loudly.

Chapter 4 – Autumn to Winter

~

Harold and Walter were at the allotment, harvesting leeks, the last of the potatoes and a few turnips. The parsnips, their leaves still fresh and green, would be best after the first frosts and, with the nights lengthening and temperatures dipping, that wouldn't be long arriving. After separating the crop, Walter putting aside some for Bert, they walked over to the winter crops of sprouting broccoli that would be ready early spring, savoy cabbages and sprouts, both intended for Christmas.

"Coming along well," said Harold.

"At least we don't have the caterpillars to contend with, not at this time of year, thank the Lord," said Walter.

"Bert's busting to be back over here," said Harold.

"Elsie is all that's stopping him," said Walter, "She's worried about him."

"It won't hurt him to rest for a few weeks, it's a rum do. You know Walter, he said he was tired a few times, exhausted was what he told me."

"We all thought it was just old age, catching up. None of us are getting any younger," said Walter.

"You don't know what's round the corner, do you?"

"A cuppa, I think," said Walter, smiling, "I got some Caribbean coffee cookies, interested?"

"Try and stop me," said Harold.

~

Chapter 4 – Autumn to Winter

Ambrose was seated in the library, a novel open on the arm of the chair and his head resting against the wing, eyes closed. Beatrice burst through the door and Ambrose woke with a start as she exclaimed, "It's there again, Ambrose."

Ambrose looked around, still confused at being woken from his slumbers as Beatrice followed with, "You were asleep, I thought you were reading."

"I was."

"It can't have been very interesting. Come into the hall, that smell is back."

Ambrose lifted himself from the chair, fully awake now and followed Beatrice. For some months she'd been complaining about an intermittent odour in the hall, and occasionally Ambrose's shower room on the lower floor. Ambrose had little sense of smell; it had disappeared shortly before he had heart problems and never returned, affecting his taste too, the reason he preferred spicy food. He explained that he couldn't detect anything but Beatrice was adamant and demanded that something be done about it.

"What do you suggest? I don't know what it is?" said Ambrose.

The stalemate continued for a few days until Ambrose was mobilised, the day he chose to clean out the garage. The integral garage adjoined the hall and downstairs shower room, though its floor was lower than that of the house. As Ambrose pulled a piece of plywood from the wall he spotted a water mark along two thirds of the length of the garage, below the

Chapter 4 – Autumn to Winter

level of the floor on the other side. He leant down to touch it; it was damp. "Water, there must be water on the other side of the wall," he said to himself. Ambrose called to Beatrice who came to investigate.

"You see, dear," she said, "I told you there was something. I think the builder in the first instance, don't you?"

"Or maybe the insurance company, they can deal with the builders, can't they?" said Ambrose.

"Leave it with me," said Beatrice, "The builders first, I think."

Ambrose didn't envy the service department of 'William Crompton, Homes of Distinction'.

~

Edwina had wandered down to Heythwaite's erstwhile bridge before her coffee house opened and found two engineers, hard-hatted and wearing high-visibility vests taking measurements using a theodolite and laser measuring devices. She stopped to talk to one of them, a woman who waved at the man on the far side of the river, speaking to him through a walkie-talkie. The consultant told Edwina that they were researching whether a temporary structure could be erected across the river until the bypass was completed to allow the road to be reopened.

"So, the bypass is going ahead?" said Edwina.

"As far as we know," said the engineer, introducing herself as Sarah, "Our firm's been asked to respond to a tender document

Chapter 4 – Autumn to Winter

and it'll include an interim solution for the bridge across the Wharfe. That's why we're here."

"A tender, what's that?" said Edwina.

"Highways are going to let a contract for the work," said Sarah, "The tender document states what's required and we need to respond with what we'll do, how we'll do it, the time frame and cost, of course."

"Sounds complicated to me," said Edwina, "I'm pleased about the bypass, that accident could have been so much worse."

"Yes, I read about it. Heythwaite's had its fair share of disasters recently, what with the fire and now the bridge," said Sarah.

"Tell me about it," said Edwina, smiling as she took her leave of the consultant, walking back up the High Street, crossing the road to open her café, hopeful that the town had turned a corner.

~

The drone had been active again since the weather improved and Daniel had used its presence to test his interceptor, as he was calling it. There'd been some complications, locking on to the drone's position had been problematic and Daniel had to improve the program he'd developed for the computer that was controlling his device. On the last occasion that he'd tested the interceptor, the tracking had worked perfectly. He'd heard the tell-tale sounds of the drone and had set up his contraption on a table in his garden, waiting for the drone to approach. Daniel

Chapter 4 – Autumn to Winter

had switched on the interceptor and started the hobby computer and its clever program. He heard the characteristic buzz of the drone, something he'd analysed so that he could use its signature frequencies to allow him to lock on to it. The interceptor woke, started to scan, panning and rotating at the same time. As the drone came into view, Daniel's device followed it and Daniel grinned. He pushed the 'fire' button briefly, sending an invisible pulse of powerful electromagnetic waves straight at the drone. Daniel watched as the aircraft wobbled and then started falling, ready to land, according to its programmed logic, before recovering as Daniel released his pressure. The operator retrieved the drone and the buzzing sound ceased.

"That'll make him think," said Daniel, to himself.

~

Four inspection holes had been cut in Beatrice and Ambrose's floor to discover the cause of the water marks in their garage and the noxious odour. The waste pipe of Ambrose's shower had been badly fitted, detaching. Water from the shower had discharged under the floors and a lake of stagnant water could be seen from the hole cut in the bathroom floor, necessitating the lifting of some ceramic tiles. One of the 'William Crompton, Homes of Distinction' service technicians was lowering a submersible pump to remove the pool of water. He'd explained to Beatrice that they would need to let the house dry out thoroughly before they repaired the damage they'd caused to find the problem. Beatrice had immediately telephoned the service manager and he'd arranged the delivery

Chapter 4 – Autumn to Winter

of three dehumidifiers and two industrial fans. All were whirring loudly, the fans directed down through the inspection holes to ventilate under the floors. The door bell rang and Beatrice, stepping around a fan and the web of electrical cables littering the floor, answered the call. On the doorstep stood a tall, balding, grey haired man, in his fifties, dressed in a smart navy suit, white shirt and striped tie.

"James McCloughlin," said the visitor, his accent Scottish, holding out his hand, "We spoke on the phone."

"Ah, yes, the service manager," said Beatrice, shaking his hand, "Do come in."

James walked through the door and examined the mayhem, saying, "It's a bit of a mess."

"Yes, it is," said Beatrice.

"It's lucky you've such a big house," said James.

"Luck is not the word I would have used," said Beatrice, glaring at the newcomer.

"Bad choice of words, I was just saying …"

"I understand your meaning," said Beatrice, interrupting, "And when you've finished, I expect my house to be in the same pristine condition that it was before this unfortunate incident."

"It'll be a few weeks, maybe a month or two, especially this time of year, before this'll be dry. I just want you to know," said James, stepping back as the pump started and dark grey liquid oozed from the end of the pipe and into the toilet basin.

Chapter 4 – Autumn to Winter

"Pristine, you understand," repeated Beatrice, staring into James's eyes making him uncomfortable.

"Of course," said James, exchanging a brief glance with one of his workmen who winked.

November

November saw the nights lengthen and days cool, accompanied by thick fogs and low temperatures. The damp made it feel much colder. Dolly and Betsy were at Edwina's Coffee House, Edwina delivering their usual order. As she placed Betsy's cherry bakewell on the table she said, "I see they've awarded the contract for the bypass."

"I was reading about that, dear," said Dolly, "I wonder when they'll start?"

"Grim time of year for that kind of work. Alastair's not happy. Some of his land has been requisitioned for the route. It's split his farm," said Betsy.

The route of the road had been published during October and, because of the collapse of the bridge, had been 'fast-tracked', as the Council spokesman had called the process. Objections had been handled speedily, unusual for the plodding bureaucracy, but made little difference to the outcome. "I spoke to one of the engineers, when they were surveying. They told me that a temporary bridge would be constructed first, then they'd start on the bypass," said Edwina.

"Are they the ones who got the contract?" said Betsy.

"Now you mention it, I don't know," said Edwina, "We'd better wait and see."

Chapter 4 – Autumn to Winter

"Did you hear about Beatrice?" said Dolly.

Edwina told Dolly that she'd met Beatrice in the High Street and Beatrice had explained, in excruciating detail, the events unfolding at their home. "They're drying out the house at the moment so Ambrose has been forced to use the guest shower room. She expects the remedial work to start in December, she told me," said Edwina.

"How the other half lives. How many bathrooms do they have?" said Betsy.

"Lots of them, Betsy," said Dolly, "I bumped into the builder the other day, that tall Scotsman you see around, what's his name?"

"James McCloughlin," said Edwina, "I see his wife occasionally, they're a nice family. He has two boys, both in their teens."

"Has he, dear? Well, he looked a bit stressed and told me that some of his clients could be difficult."

"Well, we know who he means," said Betsy, chuckling.

~

The letter from the hospital stipulated that Alastair was not to drive home after his consultations as eye drops would be used and they'd impair his vision. Alastair, stubborn as always, told Robert that 'it would be fine' but Amy was having none of it. She arranged for her mother to babysit for Kit and drove Alastair for his appointment to see the consultant ophthalmologist at Airdale Hospital, Mr Walton-Stanley. Parking had been difficult so they arrived at the appointment

Chapter 4 – Autumn to Winter

desk with five minutes to spare. Amy checked-in Alastair using an airport-style self-service kiosk and was directed to 'Zone 6'. They followed the rectangular blue-on-white signs until Alastair was in front of a reception desk where a tall, dark haired young lady was having a discussion with a porter carrying a massive pile of folders taken from a trolley containing more of the patient notes. As she placed the documents on the desk she turned to Alastair, who was clutching his appointment letter and a list of medicines that he'd been prescribed by his GP, and smiled. She took the letter from Alastair and he asked her if she wanted the list of medications too. She declined his offer, stating that a nurse would ask for it, politely telling them to wait, saying that they would be seen soon. Seated with their backs to the wall, they watched the operation of the ophthalmology department at the hospital. Elderly patients were wheeled into the room, parked against a wall and their notes given to the receptionist as the waiting area filled with people, many ancient in years, supported by walking frames or sticks. Alastair felt a fraud and, though in his sixties, did not relate to the clients of this clinic. Several times, porters walked by, pushing trolleys filled with the buff coloured folders they'd seen earlier, collecting some, delivering others, before continuing on his way like a train on a railway track, transporting documents instead of passengers.

"I thought they used computers?" said Alastair as he watched another bundle of papers being exchanged.

Amy looked up from her copy of Country Life and grinned, replying casually, "I expect they do."

Chapter 4 – Autumn to Winter

"Doesn't look like it to me," said Alastair as a young nurse, short in stature, wearing prominent dark rimmed spectacles and supporting long tightly curled hair, tied behind in a bow, appeared around the corner. Her Slavic accented voice shouted Alastair's name, as if she was reading the school register of attendance. Alastair stood and the assistant smiled as she asked Alastair to follow her. Briefly, Alastair snatched a glance at Amy who nodded. The lady showed Alastair to an examination area comprising a number of narrow rectangular sections. He entered one and was directed to a chair at the far end, above which was an illuminated box showing letters of the alphabet, arranged in rows, the letters progressively smaller towards the bottom of the frame. Alastair faced down the narrow passage as the nurse washed her hands and opened up a mirror so that Alastair could see the characters. She took a detergent wipe from a tub and cleaned a plastic frame intended to allow a patient to cover one eye at a time. Habitually, she moved slowly from foot to foot, rotating her hips as she did so. It made her appear insecure, inept, her clipped style of talking and attempt at humour reinforcing the impression. Wearing his glasses, Alastair was given a rudimentary eye test where he was asked to identify the lowest row of letters from the chart that he could see clearly. Alastair was able to read the last line of text and the assistant grinned as she said, "A full house."

Explaining that Alastair was to be given eye drops to dilate his pupils, she told him that someone else would need to administer the medication as she had not been trained and Alastair was relieved. She left Alastair alone with his thoughts for a few moments until a fulsome lady appeared with a

Chapter 4 – Autumn to Winter

trainee. She introduced herself as a staff nurse, exuding confidence as she asked again questions to identify him. She explained to Alastair what would happen next and asked for his permission for her apprentice to observe what would follow. Alastair glanced at the young nurse. She had a look of entitlement, edging on boredom, tinged with insubordination, answering the staff nurse in a tone suggesting indignation that she should be tested in such a demeaning way. Alastair smiled inwardly as he recalled his own youth and the battles he'd had with his father. Shaking her head slightly, making her light auburn bobbed style hair swirl around her neck, the staff nurse explained to Alastair that two different drops would be administered and that the second would sting, as it would when peeling onions. Her assertion was correct and Alastair blinked involuntarily, his eyes smarting and watering freely. He was then dispatched to wait outside of room thirty two and told that it would take ten to fifteen minutes for the eye medication to work, that he was not to drive until the following morning and he would need to shield his eyes from bright light, an unlikely occurrence in November in Yorkshire. Amy, hearing Alastair asking directions, joined him outside of Mr Walton-Stanley's consulting room.

"You OK?" she said.

"Can't see very well, everything's a bit blurred," said Alastair.

Fifteen minute passed before Alastair was called for his scan which was performed efficiently by a taciturn practitioner. The procedure took little time and Amy was surprised when

Chapter 4 – Autumn to Winter

Alastair reappeared. Twenty minuted later the consultant ophthalmologist appeared at the door and called Alastair's name. Mr Walton-Stanley was a short man who wore black thick rimmed spectacles and sported a shirt and corduroy trousers similar to those of Alastair. His manner was brusque, having a tendency to mutter, making it difficult for Alastair to know when he was speaking to him. He spent the first two minutes finding and examining Alastair's scan and ignored Alastair whilst he was studying the images on a display screen. Then, using a device that shone very bright light into each eye as the consultant observed through an eyepiece, Mr Walton-Stanley performed his examination and then revisited the results of the Optical Coherence Tomography scan done earlier, all without acknowledging that Alastair was present. Returning for another inspection of Alastair's eyes, the consultant added a drop of a new solution to each eye before peering into them again. Alastair noticed a yellow hue to his sight when the examination ended, his vision blurred, objects indistinct. Mr Walton-Stanley asked Alastair to wait outside until he'd completed his diagnosis and Alastair returned to Amy who stared at his face.

"Here, let me wipe that," said Amy, grabbing a fresh tissue from her bag. She used it to remove a bright yellow residue from around Alastair's eyes and showed the tissue to him, now tinged the colour of egg yolk.

"Not a wonder everything has a yellow glow," said Alastair.

"What's happening now?" said Amy.

Chapter 4 – Autumn to Winter

"Haven't a clue. I'm no wiser now than when I went in there."

After a few minutes Mr Walton-Stanley's door flung open and he again called Alastair's name. In his bumbling style, devoid of humanity, the consultant used the words 'Age Related Macular Degeneration' and handed Alastair a leaflet produced by the Royal National Institute for the Blind, a charity. The consultant had little understanding of the impact of that phrase on Alastair who was now sure that he was heading for total blindness. Alastair placed the leaflet in the envelope he was carrying, containing the list of his medications that nobody had wanted to see. Then, the consultant tried to show Alastair the images of his faulty left eye on the screen but Alastair's vision was so impaired by the medication that he was unable to view it; Mr Walton-Stanley was oblivious to Alastair's dilemma and ploughed on regardless, finishing up by asking Alastair to return in four months or should the disease progress to its 'wet form', a remark that flew straight over Alastair's head. As he was leaving, Alastair pondered that the technician who serviced his farm machinery had a better bedside manner than Mr Walton-Stanley, and told him more about symptoms and diagnosis of his mechanical equipment.

"I'm done, love, just need to book another appointment for four months time." said Alastair to Amy.

"Are you alright, Dad?" said Amy.

"I'll be fine, love. Might need a bit of help getting out of here. Can't see very well at the moment."

~

Chapter 4 – Autumn to Winter

The first anyone knew that work was about to start was when highways department cordoned off the lower end of the High Street, near the River Wharfe. Several cranes arrived, two on each side of the river, followed by a huge lorry, carrying a massive steel structure as its load. In a surprisingly short time a single-lane bridge spanned the Wharfe and construction workers were securing either end, building ramps to allow access and adding traffic lights to control vehicles on the structure, ensuring contra-flow traffic. By the end of the day, Heythwaite was open at both ends again and traffic started to flow. After he closed the opticians, Gareth wandered down the hill to watch the construction, amazed to find Daniel's van crossing the river on the new bridge. Daniel slowed, lowered the window, shouted a greeting and asked how the crossing could have arrived so speedily. Gareth shrugged and smiled, giving a thumbs up sign as Daniel sped away, up the hill towards home. Gareth walked back along the High Street to retrieve his car for the journey home. He passed the Co-operative store and popped his head inside, saying, "Anyone here?"

Alex came through from the back and Gareth could hear Iggy's drill. "Hello Gareth, nothing wrong is there, with your place?" Alex said, alarmed by the sight of his last client in Heythwaite.

"No, everything is fine, you did a great job of my practice. I wondered how it was going here, you're working late."

Chapter 4 – Autumn to Winter

"They want it done by the end of the month. The major work, roof, structural stuff, you know, was completed late, leaving us with a shorter time for the fitting out."

"Squeezed into the end, I suppose," said Gareth.

"Exactly," said Alex, "We'll do it, though, I'm sure of it, if we have to work every weekend."

"Have you seen the bridge?" said Gareth.

"No, have they started it? I saw that gigantic truck."

"Started, no they've finished, it's open," said Gareth.

Alex looked surprised and then he smiled, "Well, it'll make the journey home a bit easier." Gareth took his leave of Alex and walked up the hill, tightening his scarf against the chill of a November late afternoon. As the light faded and the street lights popped on, he glanced around. Colours were subdued, monochrome, a contrast to the vibrancy of the summer months. Was it possible that this dull grey street could again light up, escape from the melancholy of the season? Then he remembered that the festive season was around the corner, a pagan festival commandeered by the Christian religion, that brought light to a darkening world. Gareth was smiling as he reached his car, stepped inside and drove towards home, his wife and three children.

~

Elsie had permitted Bert to visit the allotment. She'd told him that he was to do no heavy lifting and to keep away from the chocolate digestives. There was little to do in any case, most of their plot dormant, resting before the miracle of spring and the flourish as each plant competed for the sunshine, water and nutrients. Walter, Harold and Bert were seated around their paraffin stove enjoying a cup of strong Yorkshire tea, their second. It was Bert's return to the fold and both Walter and Harold had asked him about the pacemaker, whether it was making a difference to him. Bert had told them that he was mindful of it at first but had soon become accustomed to the device. It was tiny and scarring from its implantation had healed well; Bert told them that he was less tired and 'on the mend'. They were pleased for their friend but something had changed, a corner turned, life's fragility confronting them squarely in the face.

December

Ryan, Jimmy's son, had arrived in Perth for a fleeting visit, returning the following day. He'd called into their office to meet with Carter's replacement, Archie, to discuss a problem client, the reason for his visit. He'd had a session with the customer later in the day. The client was important, accounting for nearly twenty percent of the Perth branch's profit. Archie accompanied Ryan and, by giving some ground, they'd resolved their customer's issues. After dropping Archie back at the office, Ryan headed for his parent's home, where he'd stay overnight. Babs had greeted him and they'd talked of family around the sparkling aquamarine pool, coffee and Tim Tam biscuits to hand. Jimmy had been playing a round of golf and they heard him open the front door as he returned. Ryan rose to greet his father and they embraced warmly in the hall before joining Babs again. After some small talk, covering ground

Chapter 4 – Autumn to Winter

already discussed between Ryan and Babs, Jimmy asked about Ryan's day and whether he'd resolved the problems. Babs excused herself so that she could prepare some food for a barbecue.

"How's Carter settling in?" said Jimmy.

"He's doing just fine, Dad. He's a real asset, not sure how I managed without him."

"Your gain is my loss."

"Is Archie not working out?" said Ryan.

"No, he's fine, but not a patch on Carter, then nobody could be. How's his rush marriage working out?"

"You know Dad, I've not seen him this happy and Angie's a firebrand, they go together well. I hope it lasts."

"That's good," said Jimmy, becoming thoughtful, "Your mum and I have been talking."

"That sounds serious."

"You remember that rumpus in Mallorca, where we lost the key after a thief took my bag?" said Jimmy.

"You bet, that's why Carter went to Yorkshire, and all that followed from the visit," said Ryan with a smile.

"Well, the safe that it opens contains something important, passed down from your grandfather, from the second world war. He was adamant that he did not want the world to see it."

"Why didn't he destroy it?" said Ryan.

"I'm not sure, son. Your grandfather rarely spoke about the war, seemed to want to put it behind him, but I've discovered a

Chapter 4 – Autumn to Winter

few things. I thought he was a war correspondent, but he was more than that, he was part of the SOE."

"What's that, dad?"

"The Special Operations Executive, he was a spy, behind enemy lines, preparing for the invasion by the allies. He left Berlin, not long before the Russians arrived."

Ryan's face was decorated with a look of surprise that morphed into shock. He knew little about World War II, and had even less interest, but this revelation about his grandfather sparked curiosity; he was seeing his grandad in a new light. "So, what's in the safe, dad?"

Jimmy walked into the house and Ryan followed as Jimmy made for his office. On his desk was a folder, which Jimmy took and opened. Inside was a bundle of papers, yellowed by the passage of time, and a buff coloured envelope. Jimmy passed the envelope to Ryan who opened it and glanced at the sepia photographs within. The face was unmistakable, even with the attempt at disguise, clearly taken in a clandestine way, the composition betraying the need for haste. Ryan turned over one of the images to reveal a date, written in his grandfather's hand: 25th April 1945.

"That's Hitler, where was it taken?"

"You haven't seen the significance of the date, have you son, why should you? It's five days before his death."

Ryan flicked through a handful of pictures, taken in sequence as the subject boarded a ship, a puzzled look spreading over Ryan's face, "He's leaving?"

Chapter 4 – Autumn to Winter

"Exactly, with your grandfather's notes, there's evidence here that Adolf Hitler escaped to South America before the end of the war."

"Then who was killed in the bunker, in Berlin?"

"Your guess is as good as mine, Ryan."

"That's dynamite, dad," said Ryan, "Why are you telling me this now?"

"We're not getting any younger, son. I want you to take hold of the baton now, keep your grandfather's papers safe for another generation. Maybe, then they can see the light of day."

"It's coming up to a century since the war, what harm would it do now?" said Ryan.

"Yes, but it's not yet a century, son. Your grandad told me to keep it under wraps for a hundred years, at least. I guess it means less to you than me but, I'm counting on you to keep my word to him, are you willing?"

"If it's that important to you, of course I will," said Ryan, staring into his father's eyes.

Jimmy stood and Ryan followed his lead. They shook hands and hugged, both unwilling to end the embrace. Jimmy broke first, smiled at his son and said, "Let's get that beer, your mum will be wondering where we are."

"I doubt it dad, there's not much that goes on that mum doesn't know about."

"You might be right about that."

~

Chapter 4 – Autumn to Winter

The Co-operative store opened its doors a week late, re-entering the whirlpool of trade with a splash, making the most of the coming festive season. The outside was festooned with lights, projecting a synchronised light show to passers by, the best on the high street, signalling that they were open for business. Inside were bargains for the season, wine, beer, citrus fruits, nuts and chocolates flavoured with exotic fruits or liquor. On the weekend of their opening, in the evening, the manager rolled out the red carpet, placing stalls outside of the shop, offering free nibbles, tea, coffee, and red or white wine to residents. Dolly and Betsy, never ones to miss out on free food or drink, each stood by one of the tables with a plate containing snacks and a glass of wine, red for Dolly and white for Betsy. Dick, sporting a walking stick, and Madge wandered by and spotted the pensioners.

"What's happening here?" said Madge.

"Free food and booze," said Betsy, "Didn't you know? It's to celebrate the Co-op's return to life."

"No, we didn't," said Dick, as one of the shop staff sauntered over and offered him and Madge a drink.

"How are you now, dear," said Dolly to Dick.

Dick explained that he was over the accident and working again. Madge butted in, telling Dolly that Dick's leg was causing him discomfort, often pain, and that Dick was far from back to normal. "You know what men are like," she said, conspiratorially, leaning towards Betsy and Dolly, "I told him to put in a claim for compensation from their insurance company."

Chapter 4 – Autumn to Winter

"Has he taken your advice, dear?" said Dolly.

"What do you think?" said Dick, smiling.

They talked of the accident, the rapidly built bridge and the bypass, plus the Christmas festivities to come. Madge explained that she and Dick were heading for the Old Oak, suggesting that Betsy and Dolly join them, but the pensioners declined, having already had several glasses of wine.

"They've become close," said Betsy as Madge and Dick crossed the road.

"Good luck to them. Dick looks much better, despite the stick, don't you think?"

"He couldn't have looked worse," said Betsy, "He's lost weight, I'm sure that helps."

A voice from the other side of the road caught their attention and Dolly waved at Beatrice who crossed to greet them. As she walked up to the store an assistant offered Beatrice a glass of wine, which she accepted and Betsy held out her glass for a refill. Dolly explained about the re-opening bash that the Co-operative were having, after which Beatrice updated them about progress on the bypass. "Work starts in the new year, just after the holiday, we've done it ladies," said Beatrice.

"Your interview clinched it Dolly," said Betsy.

"We all contributed," said Dolly, smiling at Betsy and then turning to Beatrice, "We couldn't have achieved this without your leadership, dear." Beatrice smiled and was about to speak when Dolly continued, "By the way, how are things at home after the flood?"

Chapter 4 – Autumn to Winter

"I think I have made Mr McCloughlin's life a misery," said Beatrice, a shallow smile decorating her face, "Everything is back to normal now but it took an age to dry. The house smelt musty for weeks. It was all unfortunate and, if Ambrose had listened to me earlier, we could have avoided the whole sorry mess."

"All's well that end's well, dear," said Dolly.

"Worse things happen at sea," added Betsy, grinning, the alcohol starting to affect her speech, "I think I'd better not have any more wine."

~

The infant asleep in bed, Amy was in the kitchen, pouring a beer for herself and one for Alastair. Robert was at a farmers' association meeting and would be home later. She wandered through to the lounge where the log fire was burning brightly and Alastair was seated in his favourite armchair reading a magazine. She handed him the brown ale and he smiled at her. He looked different in his new spectacles but they suited him. Amy wondered what Catherine would have thought; she would have taken it in her stride, Catherine was a farmer's wife after all, just like her. Alastair had been capricious since his visit to the eye consultant and she hadn't wanted to pressure him; he'd open up in his own time. He'd not spoken to Robert either, except to give curt answers to Robert's questions. Something was troubling him but his recalcitrance was preventing him from speaking. Alastair often said that a trouble shared was a trouble … doubled, and Amy was sure that he believed it. She

Chapter 4 – Autumn to Winter

knew differently, but the way that men and women handled their problems contrasted; she had to give him space.

"The lad's growing," said Alastair after taking a slurp of his beer, "I heard him say dada earlier."

"He can say mama too, but he's saying dada more at the moment."

They spoke of the farm, especially Alastair's beloved Wensleydale sheep. He could be loquacious about that subject and his knowledge was legend. As Alastair stoked the fire, adding another log, the kitchen door opened and Robert entered, walking through to the lounge. He greeted Amy, leaned down to kiss her, said hello to his father and returned to the kitchen to hang up his grey woodsman jacket, charcoal coloured scarf and gloves and pour himself a glass of Theakston's Old Peculiar ale. As he re-entered the lounge he mouthed 'how has it been' to Amy and she shook her head slightly, her lips conveying the words 'no different' but without speaking a word. Robert knew that they would have to wait, not realising that the wave was about to crest. It was the following day that Alastair was with Kit while Amy tended to the chickens and fetched some eggs. She walked back into the kitchen and Alastair had Kit on his knee, reading from one of the numerous children's books that they'd bought him. Tears were streaming down Alastair's face as he read to his grandson. When he spotted Amy, he tried to hide his distress but his eyes told the tale that his mouth failed to speak. Amy knelt before Alastair and Kit, saying, "Tell me what's troubling you dad."

Chapter 4 – Autumn to Winter

Alastair handed Kit to Amy and looked at her, his eyes still watery, as he took a handkerchief from his pocket and wiped his face. He smiled weakly as he said, "It's the thought of not being able to do this, read to the lad, see him grow."

"I'm here for you, dad, and so is Robert. Don't cut us out. Let me make a brew. Let's see what can be done."

Alastair nodded as Amy, with Kit in her arms, made a cup of tea and brought it to the table. She chose a seat so that she was at right angles to Alastair. Kit, spotting his grandfather, held out his arms and Alastair obliged, placing Kit on his lap. The child seemed aware of Alastair's distress and pushed his head into him, wrapping his small arms around his grandfather's middle and he remained there while Amy and Alastair spoke. The visit to the hospital consultant had confused Alastair, leaving him with more questions than answers. He'd read the leaflet from the Royal Institute for the Blind and it had frightened him. Produced in large text, it explained the progression of macular degeneration from one, then to both eyes and what to expect. The symptoms were described and it outlined the visual aids that could help, once the malady had progressed to the inevitable loss of his central sight, only peripheral vision remaining. Alastair's symptoms didn't match those described in the pamphlet but, if nothing else, Mr Walton-Stanley had been clear in his diagnosis: Alastair had 'Age Related Macular Degeneration' in his left eye and it was 'dry' rather than 'wet'. The leaflet explained that there was no cure for the dry form but that treatment needed to be applied promptly should the disease progress to its wet form. How would he know if the

Chapter 4 – Autumn to Winter

condition had worsened? Amy listened as Alastair explained his confusion and she could see that he was fearful, trying to face it alone. It was his way, close in on himself to build the strength to carry on. He was a proud man, fiercely self reliant. This ailment would strip him of his independence and it troubled him deeply. By the end of their discourse, Kit was fidgeting, ready for his morning sleep.

"I'll put him down, dad, he's tired. Stay a while, let's talk about this." said Amy. Kit was a good sleeper and was settled before Amy rejoined Alastair in the kitchen. She switched on the baby intercom and checked her offspring on the screen. Satisfied, she turned to Alastair and said, "How about giving Gareth a call if you're concerned?"

"Oh, I don't know, Amy. They all stick together don't they, medics."

"Gareth's not like that. I think he'll be honest with you. It was him who diagnosed the problem in the first place."

Alastair was mute for a moment as he stared towards the window and then said, "You might be right."

"Now?" said Amy, smiling.

Alastair grinned as he picked up his mobile, saying, "You're a hard task master Amy." Amy heard the sound of the ring tone after Alastair keyed the numbers and then the receptionist answered. Gareth was with a client but she'd have him call Alastair later.

~

Chapter 4 – Autumn to Winter

Gareth picked up the message from Alastair but wasn't able to call until the afternoon, his schedule full that day. Using his computer, he found Alastair's clinical records and looked again at the scan he'd performed during his patient's last visit. Flicking through the notes he'd made, Gareth refreshed himself with the case before he dialled Alastair's mobile number. After a few moments the call was answered and Gareth listened as Alastair told him of his consultant's visit.

"Was it Walton-Stanley you saw?" said Gareth. Alastair confirmed that he'd seen Mr Walton-Stanley and Gareth told him that he'd often had the same feedback from other patients about the consultant's manner. He asked Alastair specifically about the diagnosis, quizzing him about what Mr Walton-Stanley had told him. "You sure he said 'dry'," said Gareth and, when Alastair confirmed, Gareth continued with, "I was concerned that you might have the 'wet' form. The scan showed a raised area. It may have been fluid, that's why I referred you. There's no treatment for dry macular degeneration; most of the population have some form of wear, we just don't have another name for it and its the severity that matters." Gareth asked whether Alastair was to see the consultant again and he confirmed that he had an open appointment for four months hence. Gareth seemed pleased and suggested that Alastair find an Amsler Grid from the internet, print it out and follow the instructions. Alastair asked Gareth to spell out the unfamiliar word and he jotted it in his notebook.

Chapter 4 – Autumn to Winter

"You'll see some distortion in the grid. If it changes, come and see me immediately, or go back to the consultant," said Gareth as he explained that Alastair wasn't going blind and that the degeneration was unlikely to spread to the other eye. "I can't stop you ageing, Alastair. This is just part of growing older, like skin wrinkling, the eyes do something similar. In eye terms, the defect you have is well away from the centre and isn't impacting your sight much. Just keep an eye on it, sorry about the pun. Use the Amsler chart every day. Remember, if there's any change, don't delay. Is that alright Alastair?"

Alastair thanked Gareth and ended the call, a great weight lifted from his shoulders. Tears welled up in his eyes and one escaped from his left eye, the one with the problem. He sighed and went to find Amy. Good news was better shared.

~

"The usual is it?" said Edwina, sauntering over to the table where Dolly and Betsy were seated.

Edwina glanced at Betsy over the top of her black rimmed oversize glasses, pushed back her strawberry blond hair, and turned to face Dolly. "Not quite, Edwina," said Dolly, "tea for both of us, toasted teacake for me and …"

"Cherry bakewell for Betsy," Edwina interrupted, grinning as she turned to walk to the kitchen.

"Do you want me to do anything for Christmas?" said Betsy. With Dolly's children enjoying their life in Australia, the late Albert a fond memory, and Betsy having no immediate family, Dolly and Betsy spent Christmas together, opened their gifts,

Chapter 4 – Autumn to Winter

imbibed a few drinks, had lunch but mostly enjoyed reminiscing on the year that had passed.

"The pudding, as usual," said Dolly.

Edwina had heard the friends talking about their seasonal arrangements, so, as she returned with their order, she said, "I wasn't eavesdropping but was that Christmas you were discussing?"

"It was," said Dolly, smiling at the café proprietor.

"We always spend it together," said Betsy, taking the tray from Edwina.

"As you know, I live alone," said Edwina, peering at Betsy, because Betsy really did know everything that happened in the town, "I'm opening the café to a few invited guests and I wondered if you would join me."

"Who's coming?" said Betsy.

Dolly gave her friend a look that said 'be quiet' and interrupted with, "Is it just the three of us?"

"I've asked Walter and his friend Ludwig, who's visiting him for the season. They were at a loose end," said Edwina.

"Is there a charge?" said Betsy.

"Just a contribution for the food, at cost, that's all." said Edwina, "A little help with the cooking would be gratefully accepted too. Bring your own booze though, because I'm not licensed."

"What do you think?" said Dolly but it was clear from her demeanour, that she wanted to accept the invitation.

Chapter 4 – Autumn to Winter

"It'll be different. Why not?" said Betsy.

That's how Dolly and Betsy found themselves walking up an empty high street on Christmas day towards Edwina's Coffee House. The day was bitterly cold, with a strong easterly wind blowing, but the sun shone and it was bright. Betsy dressed as she always did, making no allowances for the festivities. Dolly, on the other hand, had perfectly coiffured hair, classily applied make-up and wore a royal blue blouse with contrasting skirt. She'd donned her best coat of the finest Yorkshire wool. Entering the café, Dolly shouted a greeting to indicate their presence, and Edwina popped her head around the door of the kitchen. "My, you look nice. Hope you've an apron, we don't want to spoil your clothes."

"Are we the first?" said Dolly, smiling as she placed the bag she was carrying on a table. She pulled out two pinafores, one for her and one for Betsy, a couple of bottles of stout for Betsy, a bottle of sherry and one of wine.

"Walter and Ludwig will be here soon. They're bringing the bird. They cooked it slow over night, so it should be succulent. Just the vegetables for us to finish. I've made a start."

"Hope they've pigs-in-blankets, and gravy," said Betsy.

"Of course, they're bringing them both." said Edwina, "Have you the pudding?"

Betsy pulled the Marks and Spencer, Christmas pudding from her bag as she said, "It's cooked. Just needs heating through."

"We're forgetting our manners," said Dolly, "Merry Christmas, Edwina."

Chapter 4 – Autumn to Winter

There was a ding sound and the ladies turned around as Walter and his friend, also well into his pension years, walked through the door. Walter was carrying a large plastic box with an ill-fitting lid, and Ludwig balanced a metal plate stacked with sausages wrapped in bacon in one hand and a bag in the other. "Here, let me help you," said Dolly, moving forward to relieve Ludwig of the plate as Edwina took the box from Walter.

"Oh, that smells lovely," said Edwina.

"You've got gravy?" said Betsy.

"It's in a jug, in the box, a Caribbean speciality," said Walter, grinning.

"Merry Christmas," said Edwina as the group clumsily exchanged greetings.

"A drink, perhaps?" said Ludwig.

"Don't mind if I do. Mine's a stout," said Betsy.

She leaned over to Dolly, winked and smiled as she whispered, "Might be a good do, Dolly."

Dolly gave her friend a mischievous glance and a broad grin started to decorate her face.

~

"It's been a funny old year," said Dolly, "One way or another."

It was new years eve, the last day of a year of mixed fortunes. Betsy was with Dolly and would stay the night, Dolly having made up the bed for her in the guest room. It was nearing

Chapter 4 – Autumn to Winter

midnight and they stood by the bay window in Dolly's lounge looking over the High Street, watching a few revellers travelling from house to house. The air was crisp and a frost clung to the trees and whitened the ground. Houses opposite were decorated with lights from the festive season, now nearly over.

"The break-in's, Dick's accident, that dreadful storm, the bridge collapsing," said Dolly, nursing a glass of fizzy white wine, "and that drone, though it's stopped for the winter."

"Good parts too, Dolly. Let's think of those at new year. Alastair has a new grandson and our trip to Australia, I'll never forget that."

"It was wonderful, Betsy. Angie started a new life there too."

"I wonder how she's doing? If this was a novel, the next one would be about their life together, a real love story, and probably find out what that blasted drone was up to."

"You old romantic, I never thought you had it in you Betsy."

"There's life in the old dog yet," said Betsy as the Church bells started ringing announcing the start of the new year.

"Happy new year, dear," said Dolly.

Betsy lifted her glass of stout into the air and smiled at her old friend, "Here's to a few more Dolly, and more adventures too."

Last Word

We at Wise Grey Owl hope you've enjoyed **Four Seasons of Heythwaite** and that you'll be back for more Yorkshire adventures from our author **Annie Eileen Rogers**.

Reviews are important to our writers so please, if you've enjoyed the novel, **leave a review**. If you didn't, please tell us and we'll pass the comments on to the author who will cry a little but use your feedback to improve, because that's what writers do.

Please visit our web site at www.wisegreyowl.co.uk or www.wisegrayowl.com where you'll find books from authors you may not have met before, but will want to meet again. If you are a writer, list your book there for free or advertise with us – it's like a donation, but you receive something in return.

Printed in Poland
by Amazon Fulfillment
Poland Sp. z o.o., Wrocław